DISNEY
PRINCESS

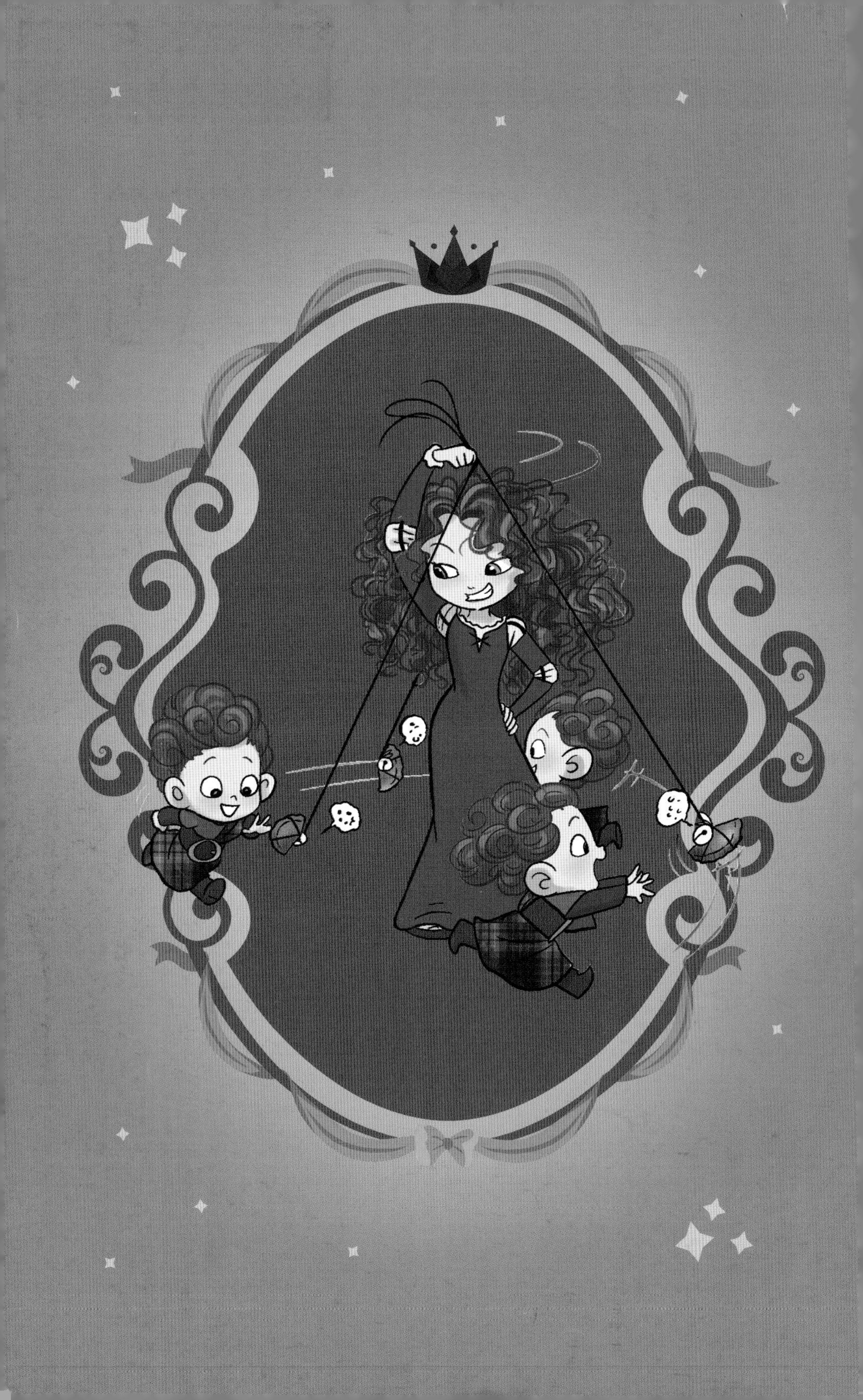

DISNEY PRINCESS

Make Way for Fun

Script and Illustration by
Amy Mebberson

Lettering by
AndWorld Design

Cover Art by
Amy Mebberson

Dark Horse Books

Before we jump
into stories with the
Disney Princesses, let's take
a moment to learn some
quick key details about a
few of them with these very
informative *infographics*!

**Presenting Jasmine,
Moana, and Merida . . .**

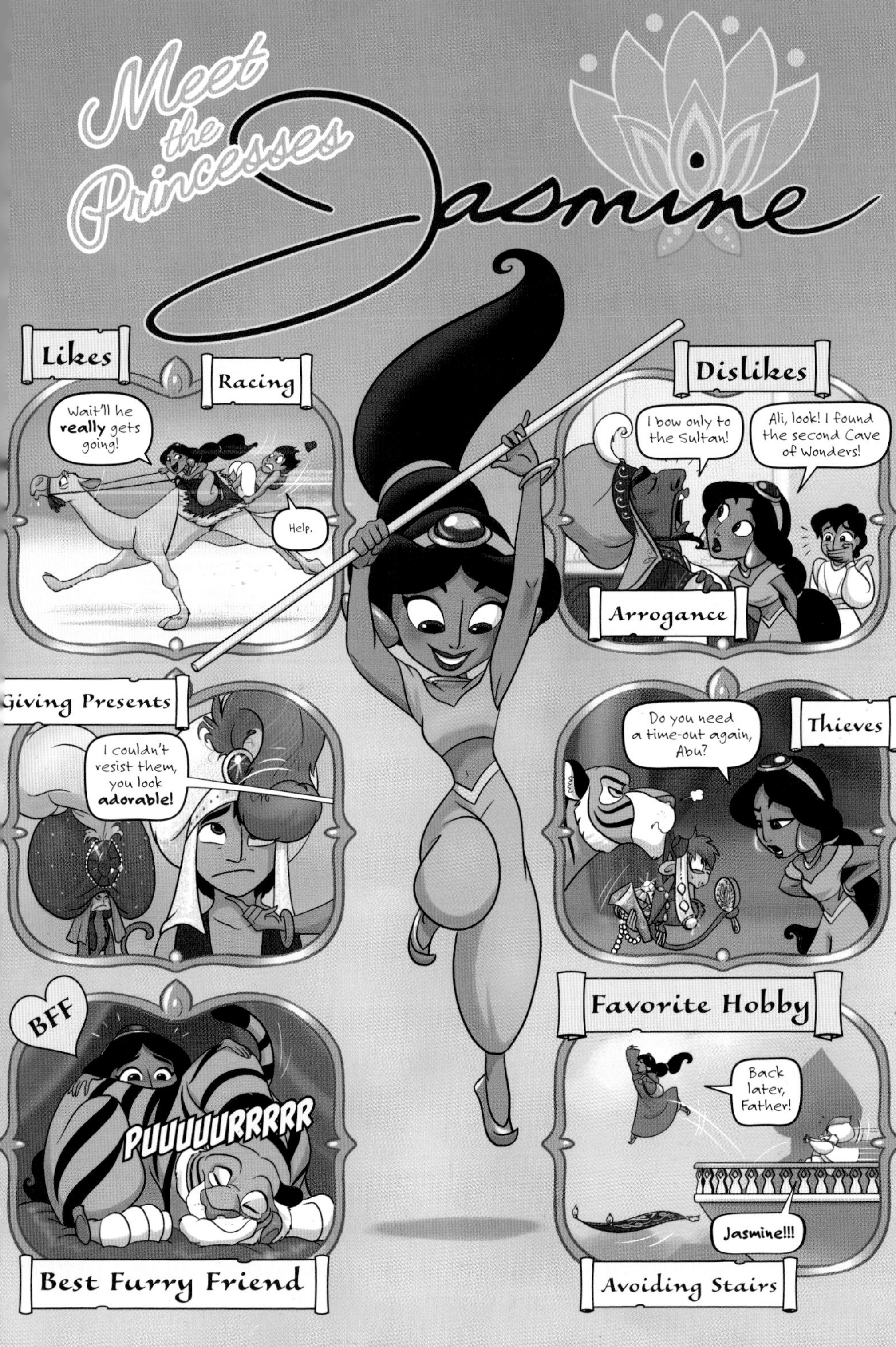

Meet the Princesses
Jasmine
Likes
Racing
Wait'll he **really** gets going!
Help.
Dislikes
Arrogance
I bow only to the Sultan!
Ali, look! I found the second Cave of Wonders!
Giving Presents
I couldn't resist them, you look **adorable!**
Thieves
Do you need a time-out again, Abu?
BFF
PUUUUURRRRR
Best Furry Friend
Favorite Hobby
Back later, Father!
Jasmine!!!
Avoiding Stairs

Meet the Princesses
Moana

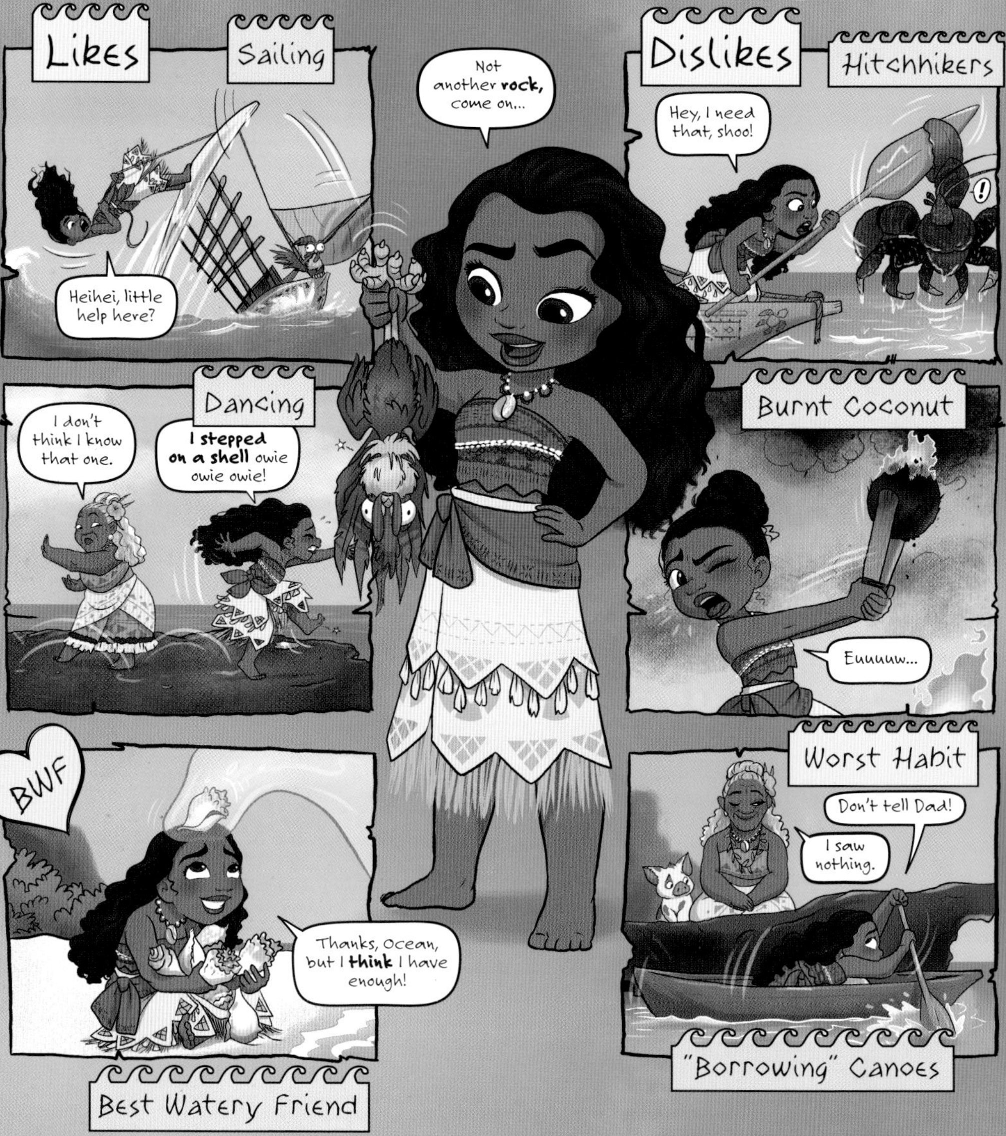

Likes
Sailing
Heihei, little help here?
Not another **rock**, come on...
Dislikes
Hitchhikers
Hey, I need that, shoo!
!
Dancing
I don't think I know that one.
I stepped on a shell owie owie owie!
Burnt Coconut
Euuuuw...
BWF
Thanks, Ocean, but I **think** I have enough!
Best Watery Friend
Worst Habit
Don't tell Dad!
I saw nothing.
"Borrowing" Canoes

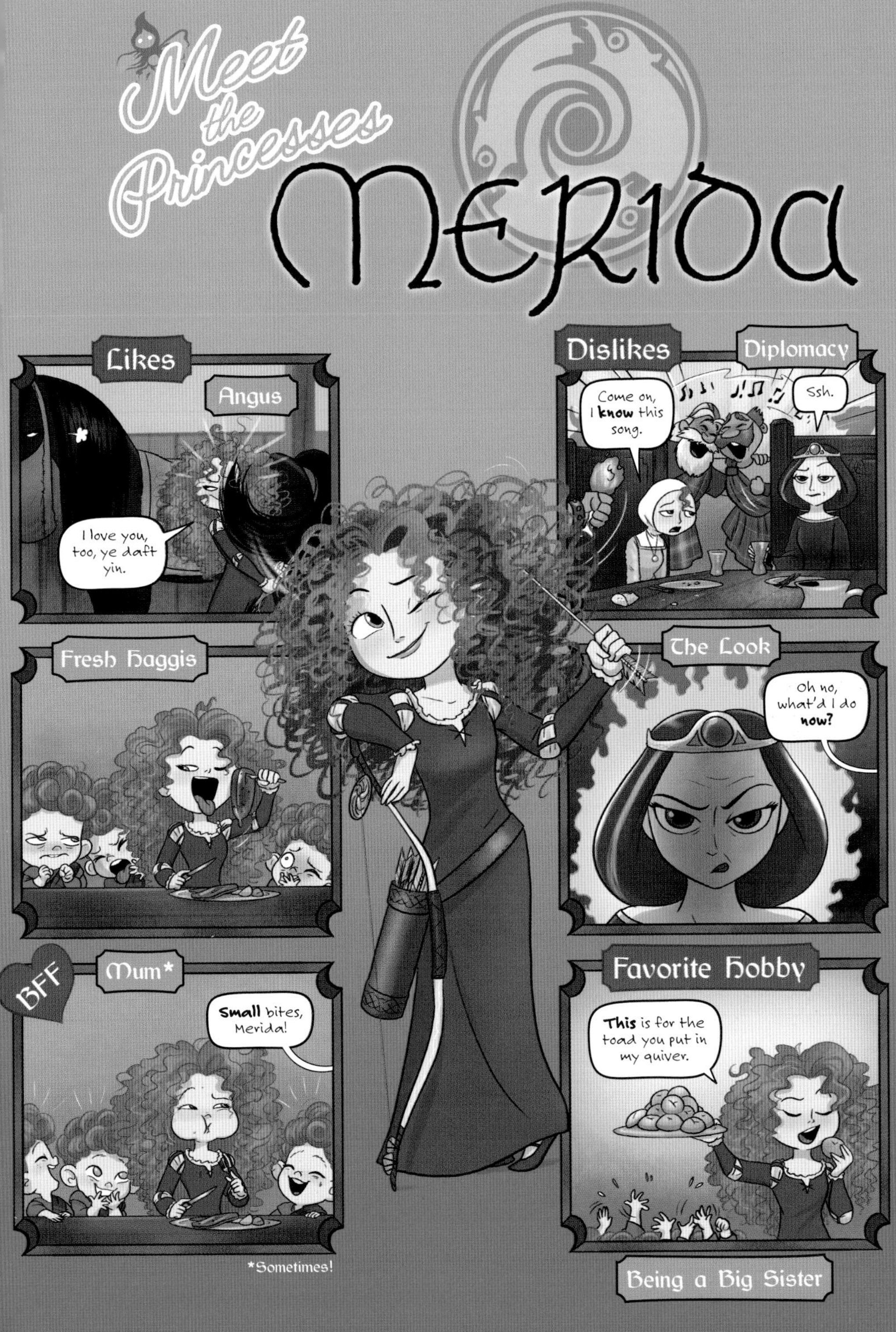

Meet the Princesses
MERIDA
Likes
Angus
I love you, too, ye daft yin.
Dislikes
Diplomacy
Come on, I **know** this song.
Ssh.
Fresh Haggis
The Look
Oh no, what'd I do **now?**
BFF
Mum*
Small bites, Merida!
*Sometimes!
Favorite Hobby
This is for the toad you put in my quiver.
Being a Big Sister

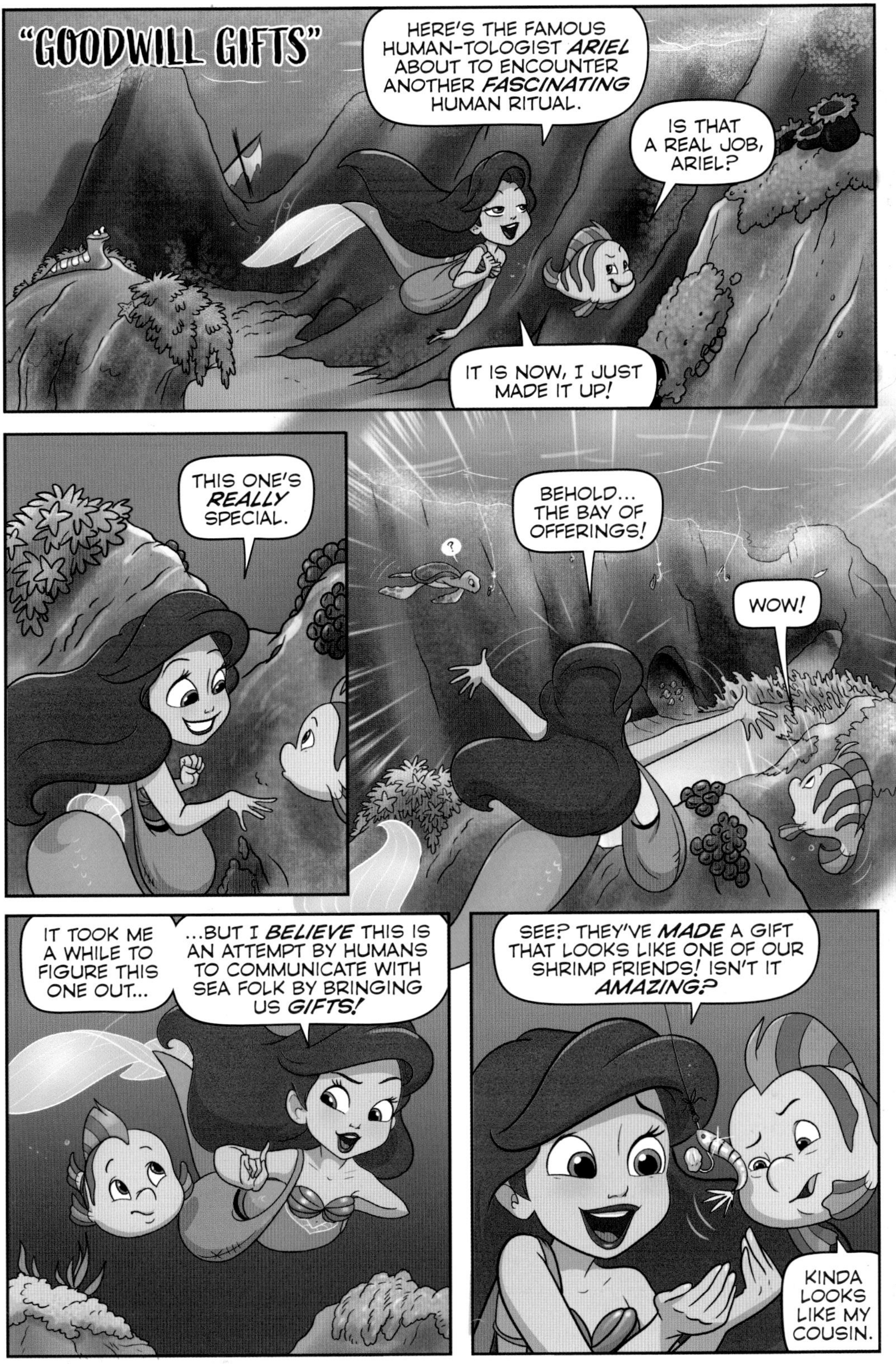
"GOODWILL GIFTS"
HERE'S THE FAMOUS HUMAN-TOLOGIST ARIEL ABOUT TO ENCOUNTER ANOTHER FASCINATING HUMAN RITUAL.
IS THAT A REAL JOB, ARIEL?
IT IS NOW, I JUST MADE IT UP!
THIS ONE'S REALLY SPECIAL.
BEHOLD... THE BAY OF OFFERINGS!
?
WOW!
IT TOOK ME A WHILE TO FIGURE THIS ONE OUT...
...BUT I BELIEVE THIS IS AN ATTEMPT BY HUMANS TO COMMUNICATE WITH SEA FOLK BY BRINGING US GIFTS!
SEE? THEY'VE MADE A GIFT THAT LOOKS LIKE ONE OF OUR SHRIMP FRIENDS! ISN'T IT AMAZING?
KINDA LOOKS LIKE MY COUSIN.

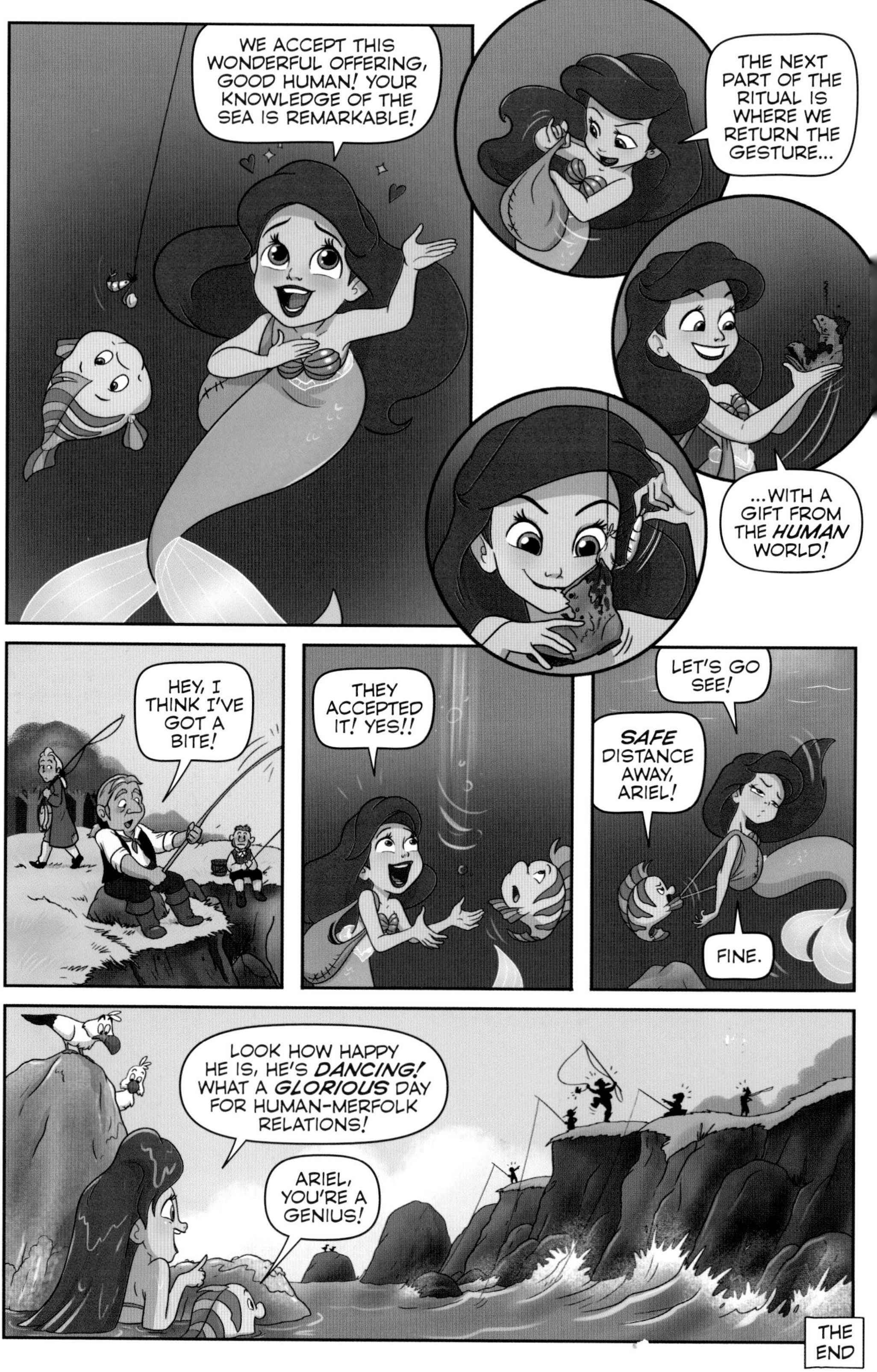
WE ACCEPT THIS WONDERFUL OFFERING, GOOD HUMAN! YOUR KNOWLEDGE OF THE SEA IS REMARKABLE!
THE NEXT PART OF THE RITUAL IS WHERE WE RETURN THE GESTURE...
...WITH A GIFT FROM THE *HUMAN* WORLD!
HEY, I THINK I'VE GOT A BITE!
THEY ACCEPTED IT! YES!!
LET'S GO SEE!
SAFE DISTANCE AWAY, ARIEL!
FINE.
LOOK HOW HAPPY HE IS, HE'S *DANCING!* WHAT A *GLORIOUS* DAY FOR HUMAN-MERFOLK RELATIONS!
ARIEL, YOU'RE A GENIUS!
THE END

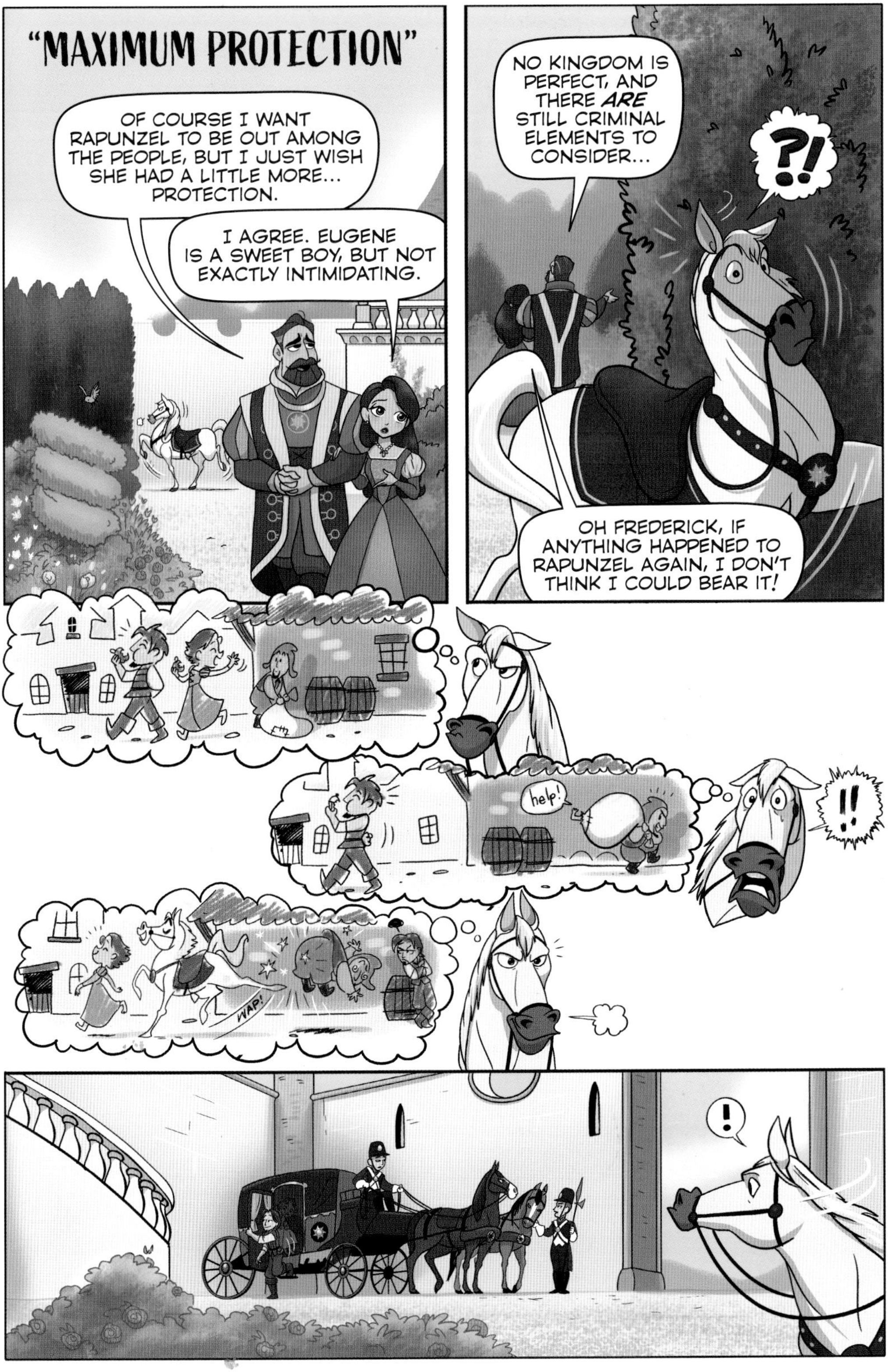
"MAXIMUM PROTECTION"
OF COURSE I WANT RAPUNZEL TO BE OUT AMONG THE PEOPLE, BUT I JUST WISH SHE HAD A LITTLE MORE... PROTECTION.
I AGREE. EUGENE IS A SWEET BOY, BUT NOT EXACTLY INTIMIDATING.
NO KINGDOM IS PERFECT, AND THERE ARE STILL CRIMINAL ELEMENTS TO CONSIDER...
?!
OH FREDERICK, IF ANYTHING HAPPENED TO RAPUNZEL AGAIN, I DON'T THINK I COULD BEAR IT!
help!
!!
WAP!
!

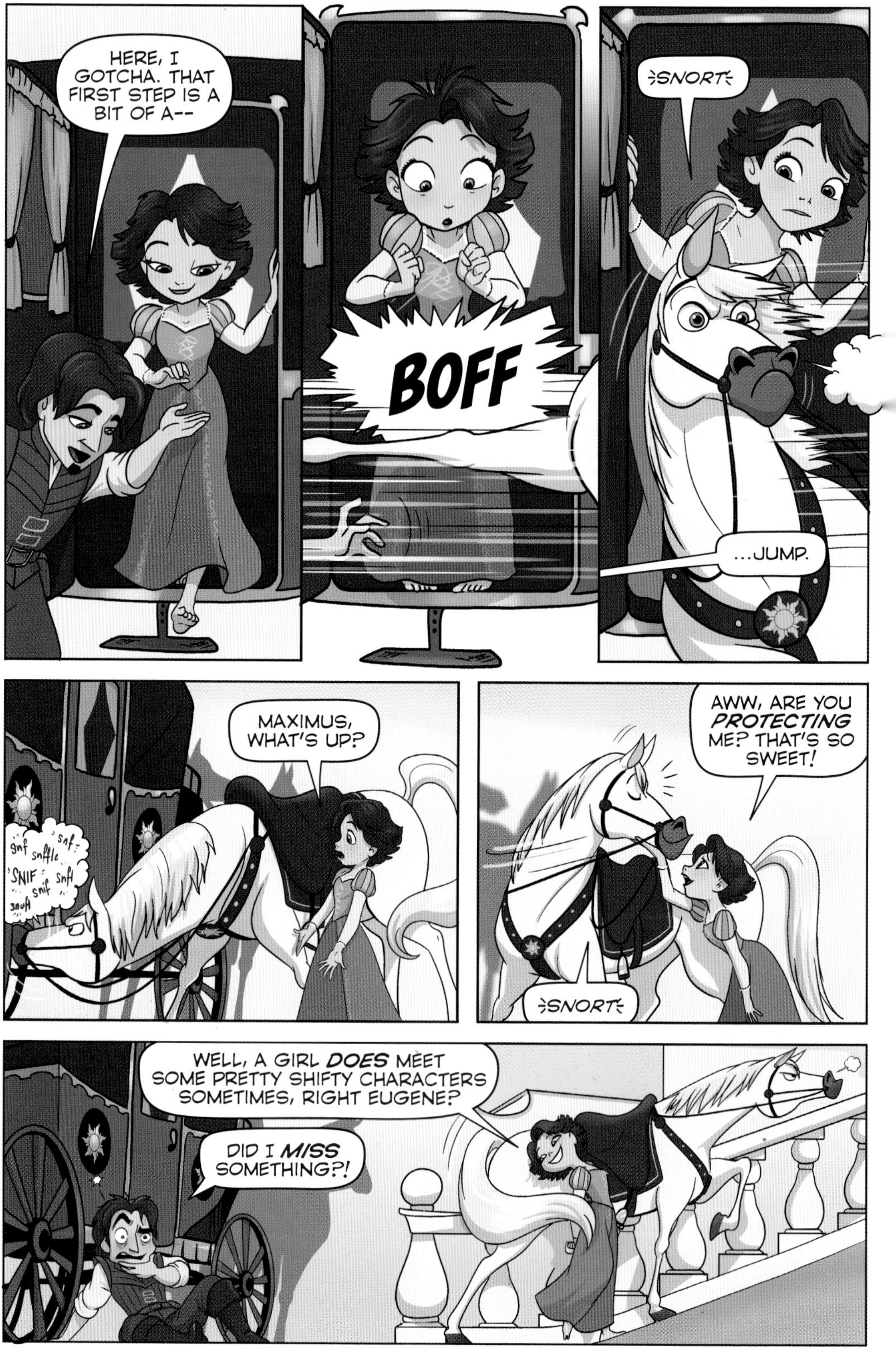
HERE, I GOTCHA. THAT FIRST STEP IS A BIT OF A--
BOFF
SNORT
...JUMP.
MAXIMUS, WHAT'S UP?
snf snffle snf SNIF snfl snif snuff
AWW, ARE YOU *PROTECTING* ME? THAT'S SO SWEET!
SNORT
WELL, A GIRL *DOES* MEET SOME PRETTY SHIFTY CHARACTERS SOMETIMES, RIGHT EUGENE?
DID I *MISS* SOMETHING?!

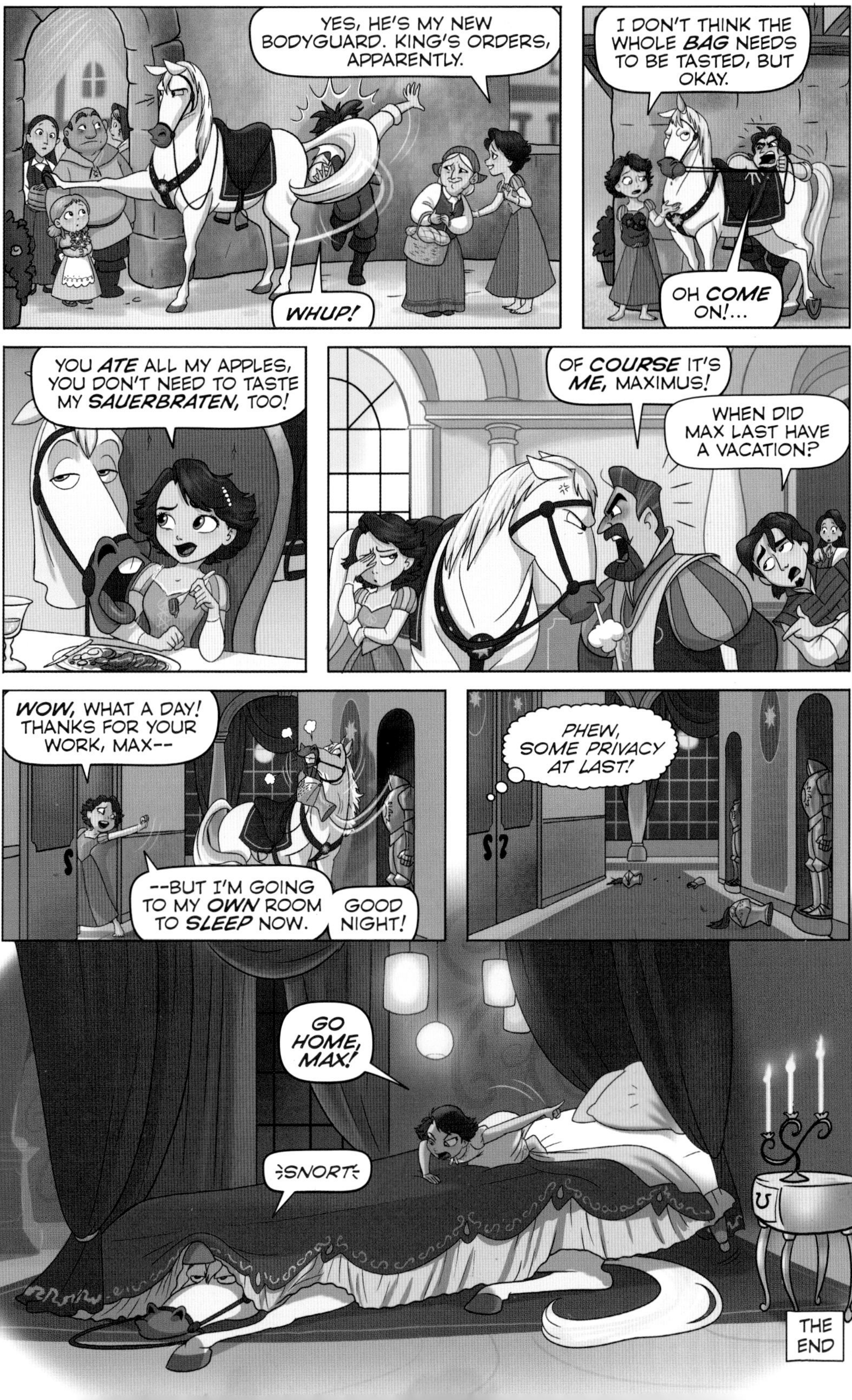
YES, HE'S MY NEW BODYGUARD. KING'S ORDERS, APPARENTLY.
WHUP!
I DON'T THINK THE WHOLE BAG NEEDS TO BE TASTED, BUT OKAY.
OH COME ON!...
YOU ATE ALL MY APPLES, YOU DON'T NEED TO TASTE MY SAUERBRATEN, TOO!
OF COURSE IT'S ME, MAXIMUS!
WHEN DID MAX LAST HAVE A VACATION?
WOW, WHAT A DAY! THANKS FOR YOUR WORK, MAX--
--BUT I'M GOING TO MY OWN ROOM TO SLEEP NOW.
GOOD NIGHT!
PHEW, SOME PRIVACY AT LAST!
GO HOME, MAX!
SNORT
THE END

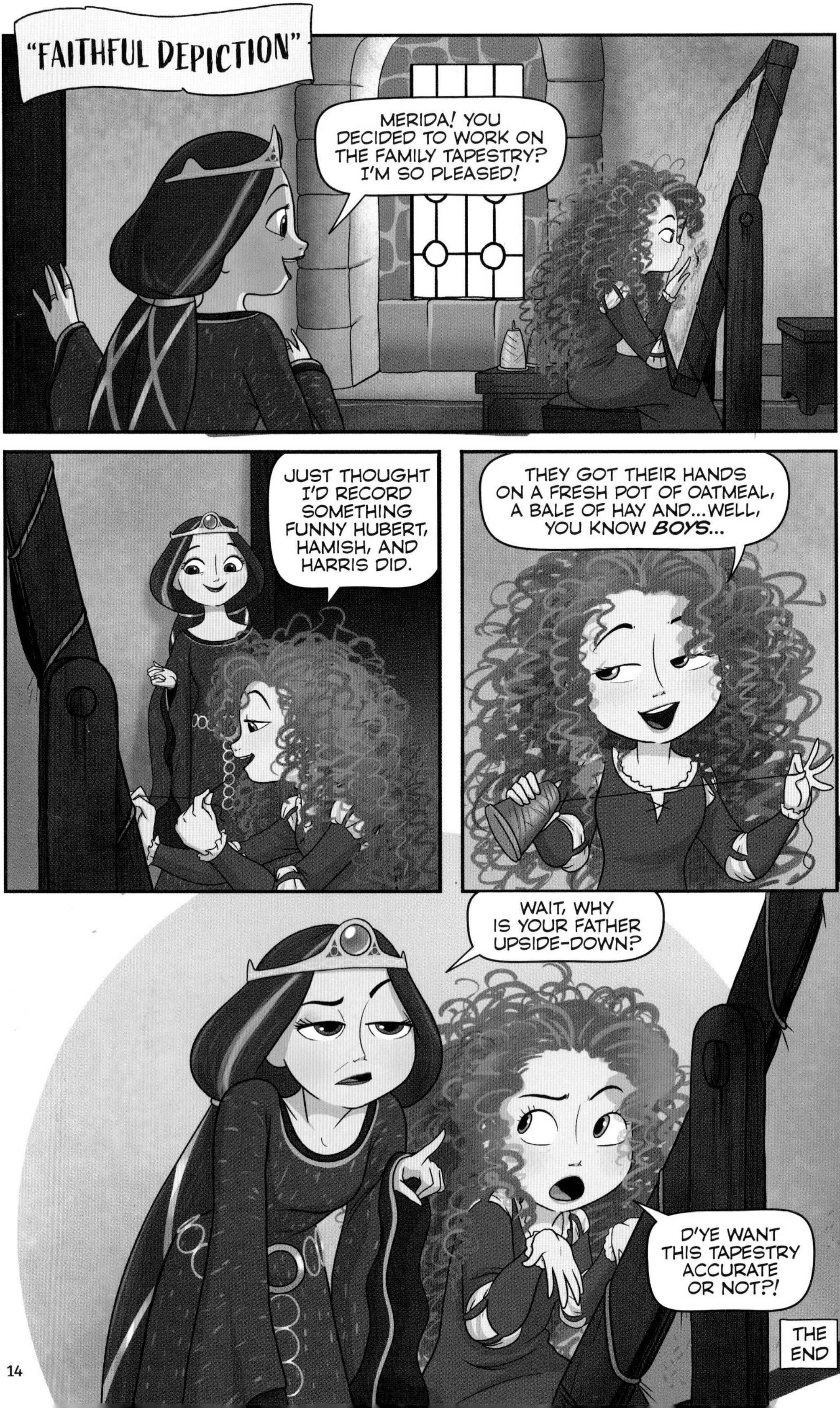
"FAITHFUL DEPICTION"
MERIDA! YOU DECIDED TO WORK ON THE FAMILY TAPESTRY? I'M SO PLEASED!
JUST THOUGHT I'D RECORD SOMETHING FUNNY HUBERT, HAMISH, AND HARRIS DID.
THEY GOT THEIR HANDS ON A FRESH POT OF OATMEAL, A BALE OF HAY AND...WELL, YOU KNOW *BOYS*...
WAIT, WHY IS YOUR FATHER UPSIDE-DOWN?
D'YE WANT THIS TAPESTRY ACCURATE OR NOT?!
THE END

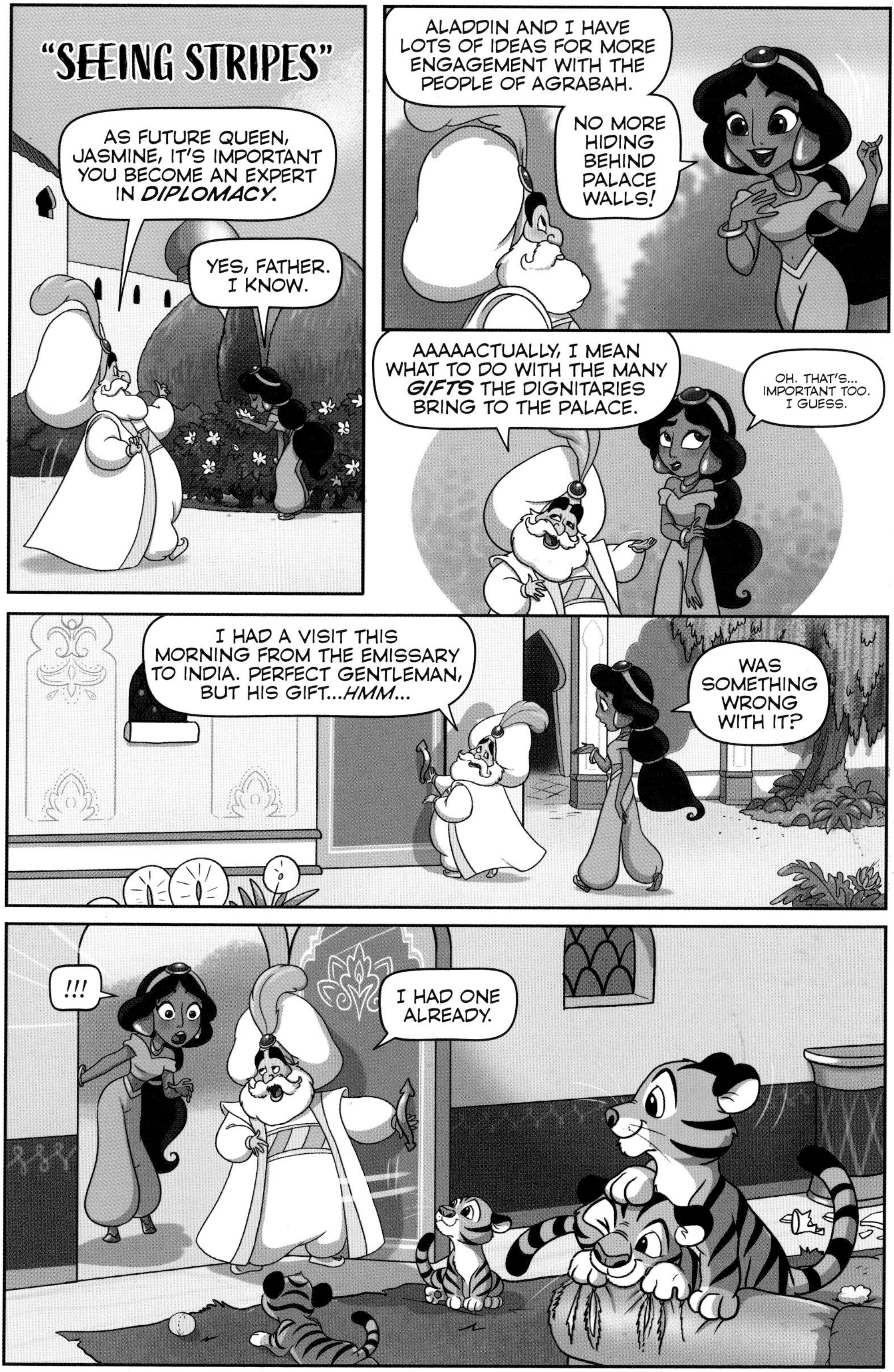
"SEEING STRIPES"
AS FUTURE QUEEN, JASMINE, IT'S IMPORTANT YOU BECOME AN EXPERT IN DIPLOMACY.
YES, FATHER. I KNOW.
ALADDIN AND I HAVE LOTS OF IDEAS FOR MORE ENGAGEMENT WITH THE PEOPLE OF AGRABAH.
NO MORE HIDING BEHIND PALACE WALLS!
AAAAACTUALLY, I MEAN WHAT TO DO WITH THE MANY GIFTS THE DIGNITARIES BRING TO THE PALACE.
OH. THAT'S... IMPORTANT TOO. I GUESS.
I HAD A VISIT THIS MORNING FROM THE EMISSARY TO INDIA. PERFECT GENTLEMAN, BUT HIS GIFT...HMM...
WAS SOMETHING WRONG WITH IT?
!!!
I HAD ONE ALREADY.

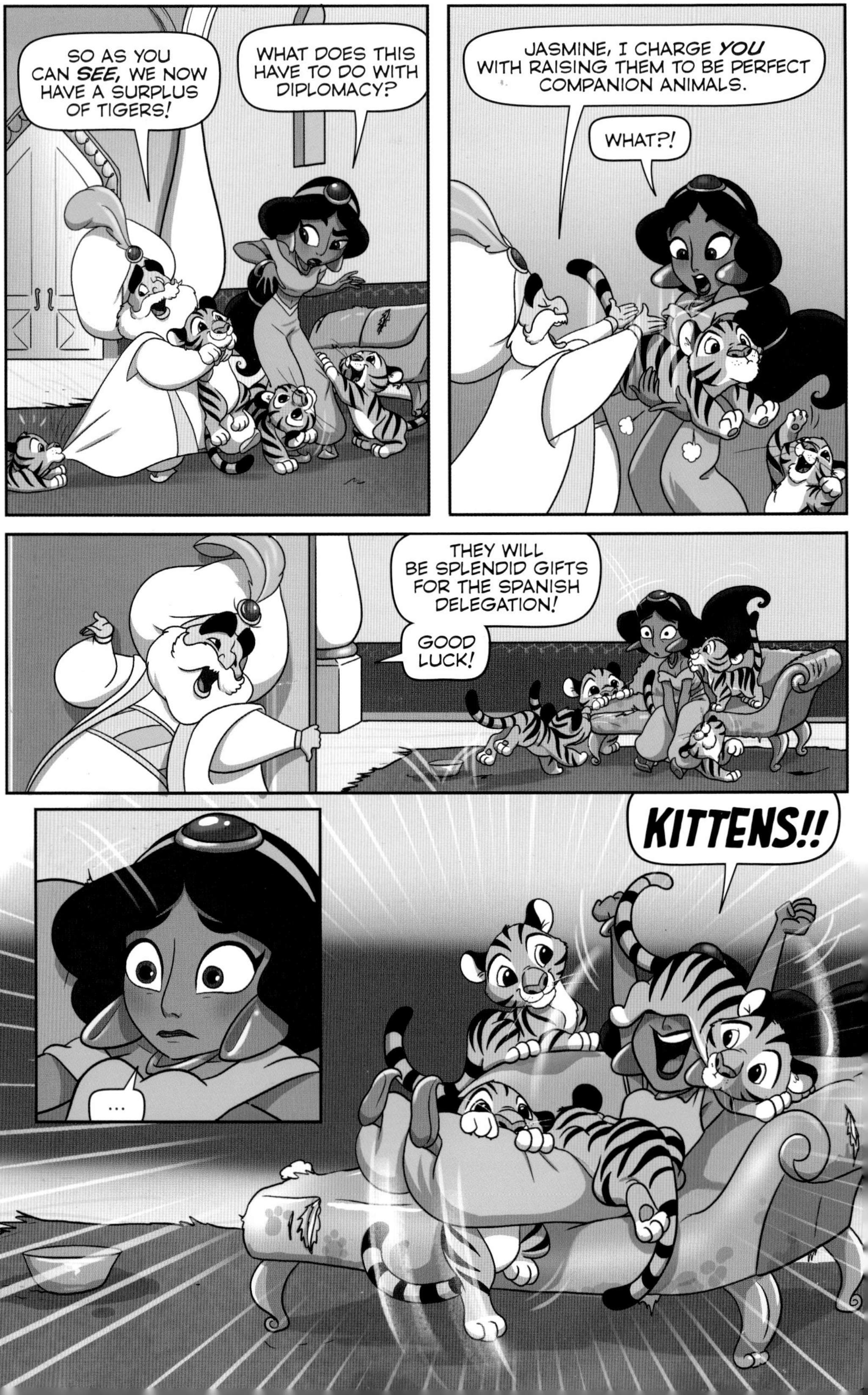
SO AS YOU CAN SEE, WE NOW HAVE A SURPLUS OF TIGERS!
WHAT DOES THIS HAVE TO DO WITH DIPLOMACY?
JASMINE, I CHARGE YOU WITH RAISING THEM TO BE PERFECT COMPANION ANIMALS.
WHAT?!
THEY WILL BE SPLENDID GIFTS FOR THE SPANISH DELEGATION!
GOOD LUCK!
...
KITTENS!!

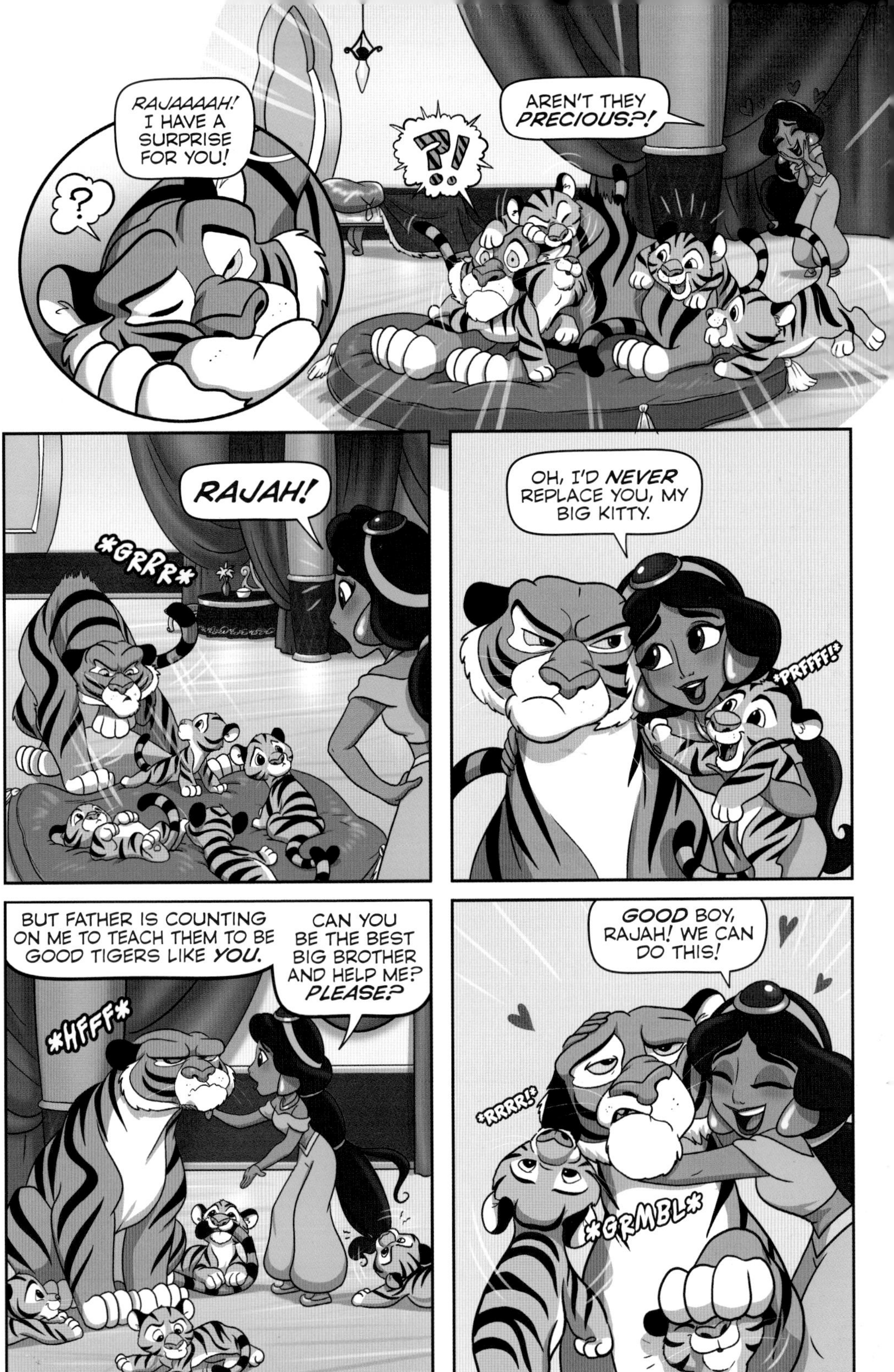
RAJAAAAH! I HAVE A SURPRISE FOR YOU!
?
?!
AREN'T THEY PRECIOUS?!
RAJAH!
GRRR
OH, I'D NEVER REPLACE YOU, MY BIG KITTY.
PRFFF!
BUT FATHER IS COUNTING ON ME TO TEACH THEM TO BE GOOD TIGERS LIKE YOU.
CAN YOU BE THE BEST BIG BROTHER AND HELP ME? PLEASE?
HFFF
GOOD BOY, RAJAH! WE CAN DO THIS!
RRRR!
GRMBL

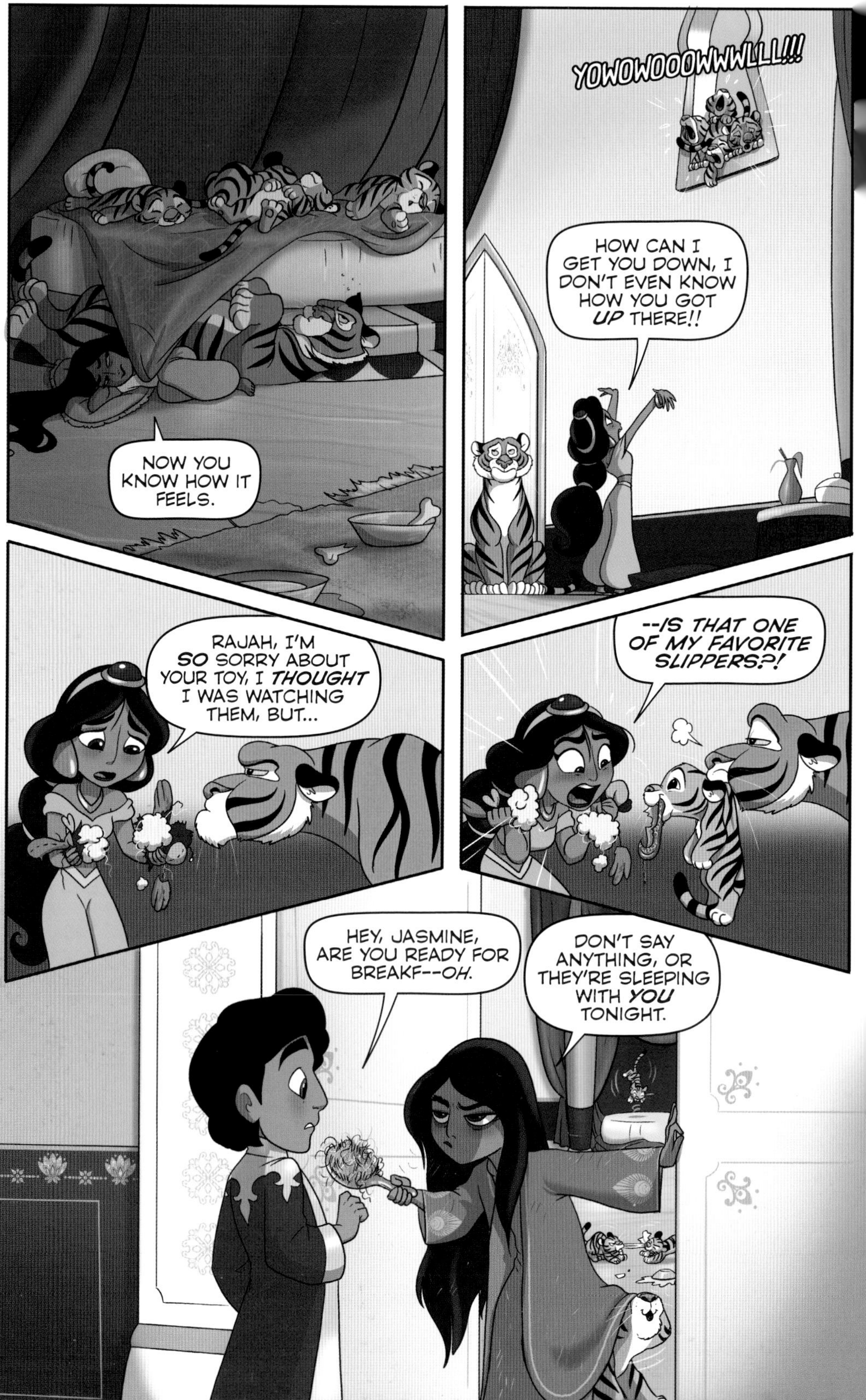
NOW YOU KNOW HOW IT FEELS.
YOWOWOOOWWWLLL!!!
HOW CAN I GET YOU DOWN, I DON'T EVEN KNOW HOW YOU GOT *UP* THERE!!
RAJAH, I'M *SO* SORRY ABOUT YOUR TOY, I *THOUGHT* I WAS WATCHING THEM, BUT...
--IS THAT ONE OF MY FAVORITE SLIPPERS?!
HEY, JASMINE, ARE YOU READY FOR BREAKF--*OH*.
DON'T SAY ANYTHING, OR THEY'RE SLEEPING WITH *YOU* TONIGHT.

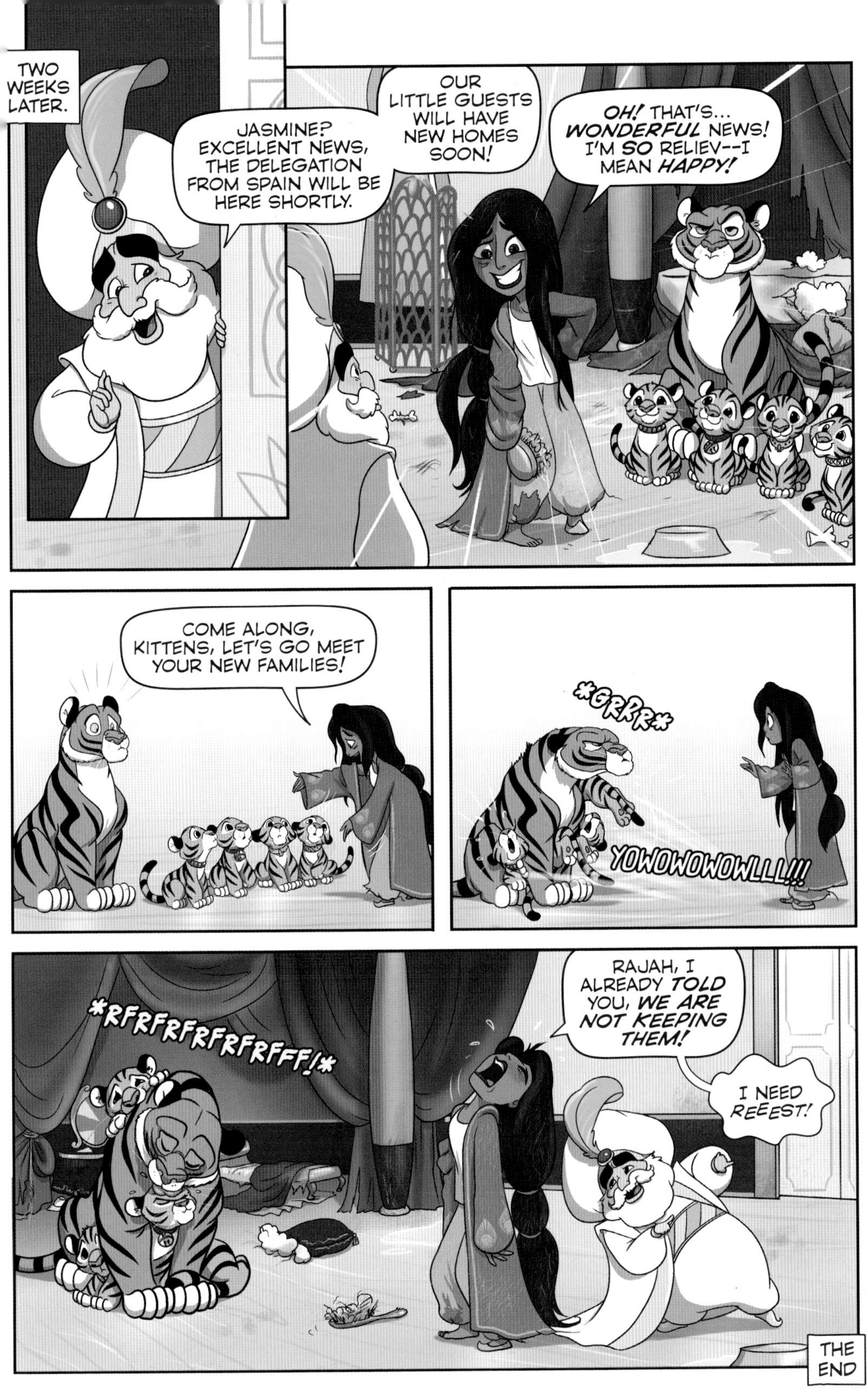
TWO WEEKS LATER.
JASMINE? EXCELLENT NEWS, THE DELEGATION FROM SPAIN WILL BE HERE SHORTLY.
OUR LITTLE GUESTS WILL HAVE NEW HOMES SOON!
OH! THAT'S... WONDERFUL NEWS! I'M SO RELIEV--I MEAN HAPPY!
COME ALONG, KITTENS, LET'S GO MEET YOUR NEW FAMILIES!
GRRR
YOWOWOWOWLLL!!!
RFRFRFRFRFRFFF!
RAJAH, I ALREADY TOLD YOU, WE ARE NOT KEEPING THEM!
I NEED REEEST!
THE END

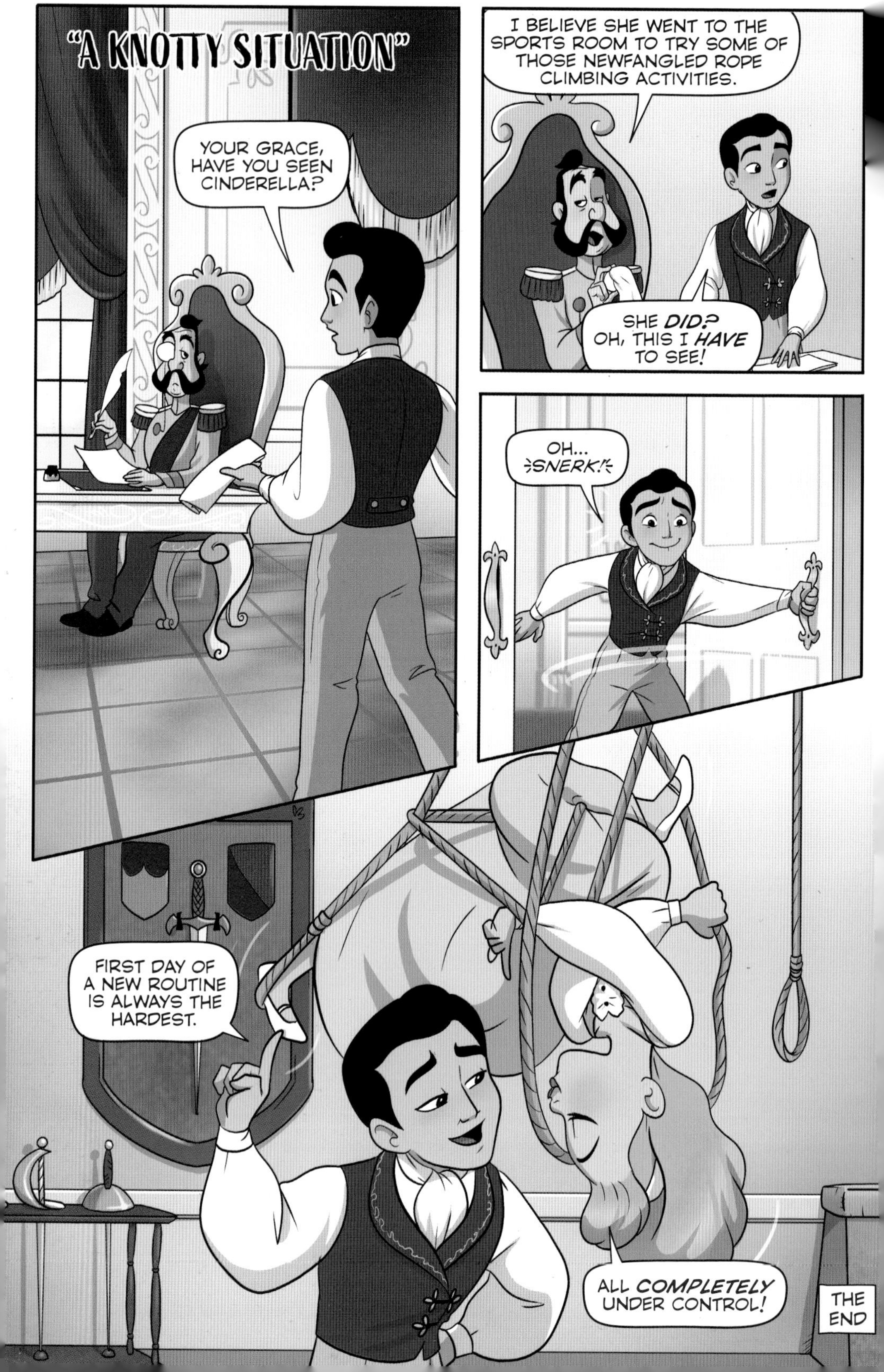
"A KNOTTY SITUATION"
YOUR GRACE, HAVE YOU SEEN CINDERELLA?
I BELIEVE SHE WENT TO THE SPORTS ROOM TO TRY SOME OF THOSE NEWFANGLED ROPE CLIMBING ACTIVITIES.
SHE *DID?* OH, THIS I *HAVE* TO SEE!
OH... *SNERK!*
FIRST DAY OF A NEW ROUTINE IS ALWAYS THE HARDEST.
ALL **COMPLETELY** UNDER CONTROL!
THE END

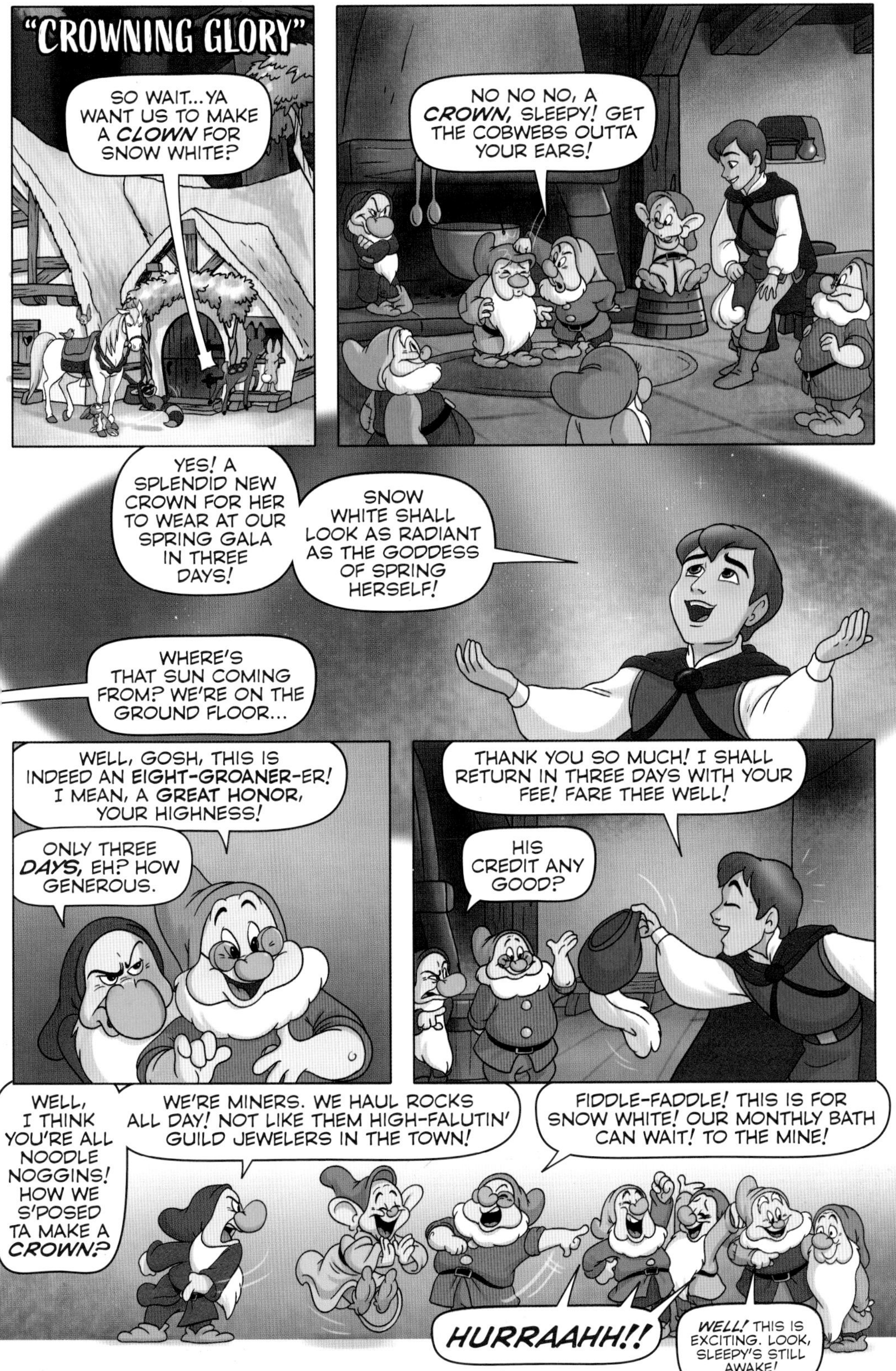

"CROWNING GLORY"
SO WAIT...YA WANT US TO MAKE A CLOWN FOR SNOW WHITE?
NO NO NO, A CROWN, SLEEPY! GET THE COBWEBS OUTTA YOUR EARS!
YES! A SPLENDID NEW CROWN FOR HER TO WEAR AT OUR SPRING GALA IN THREE DAYS!
SNOW WHITE SHALL LOOK AS RADIANT AS THE GODDESS OF SPRING HERSELF!
WHERE'S THAT SUN COMING FROM? WE'RE ON THE GROUND FLOOR...
WELL, GOSH, THIS IS INDEED AN EIGHT-GROANER-ER! I MEAN, A GREAT HONOR, YOUR HIGHNESS!
ONLY THREE DAYS, EH? HOW GENEROUS.
THANK YOU SO MUCH! I SHALL RETURN IN THREE DAYS WITH YOUR FEE! FARE THEE WELL!
HIS CREDIT ANY GOOD?
WELL, I THINK YOU'RE ALL NOODLE NOGGINS! HOW WE S'POSED TA MAKE A CROWN?
WE'RE MINERS. WE HAUL ROCKS ALL DAY! NOT LIKE THEM HIGH-FALUTIN' GUILD JEWELERS IN THE TOWN!
FIDDLE-FADDLE! THIS IS FOR SNOW WHITE! OUR MONTHLY BATH CAN WAIT! TO THE MINE!
HURRAAHH!!
WELL! THIS IS EXCITING. LOOK, SLEEPY'S STILL AWAKE!

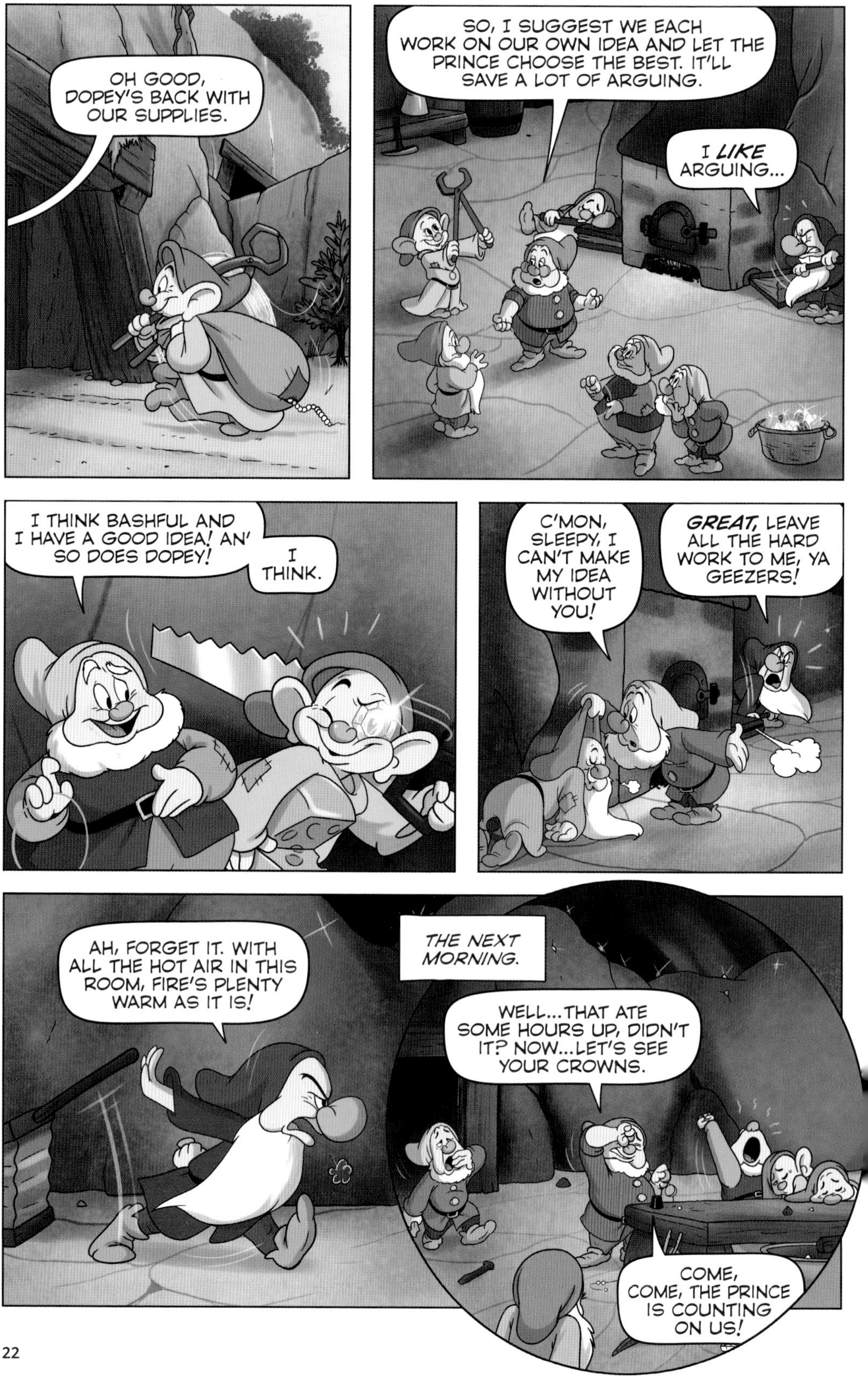
OH GOOD, DOPEY'S BACK WITH OUR SUPPLIES.
SO, I SUGGEST WE EACH WORK ON OUR OWN IDEA AND LET THE PRINCE CHOOSE THE BEST. IT'LL SAVE A LOT OF ARGUING.
I *LIKE* ARGUING...
I THINK BASHFUL AND I HAVE A GOOD IDEA! AN' SO DOES DOPEY!
I THINK.
C'MON, SLEEPY, I CAN'T MAKE MY IDEA WITHOUT YOU!
GREAT, LEAVE ALL THE HARD WORK TO ME, YA GEEZERS!
AH, FORGET IT. WITH ALL THE HOT AIR IN THIS ROOM, FIRE'S PLENTY WARM AS IT IS!
THE NEXT MORNING.
WELL...THAT ATE SOME HOURS UP, DIDN'T IT? NOW...LET'S SEE YOUR CROWNS.
COME, COME, THE PRINCE IS COUNTING ON US!

OH! WELL, THAT'S...

HMMM...

OH MY... ER...

GOSH, I DUNNO...SOMETHING ABOUT EACH OF THESE DOESN'T FEEL QUITE RIGHT. LIKE WE'RE MISSING SOMETHING.

BUT, Y'KNOW, WE DID OUR BEST, FELLAS. A-AND SNOW WHITE WOULD SAY THAT'S WHAT'S IMPORTANT!

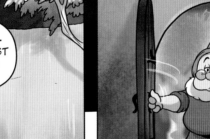

I JUST HOPE THE PRINCE UNDERSTANDS, TOO.

C'MON, LET'S GO GET SOME SHUT-EYE. MAYBE WE'RE JUST TOO TIRED TO THINK ANYMORE RIGHT NOW.

≶GASP≶

THUNK ≶OOF≶ ≶ERF!≶

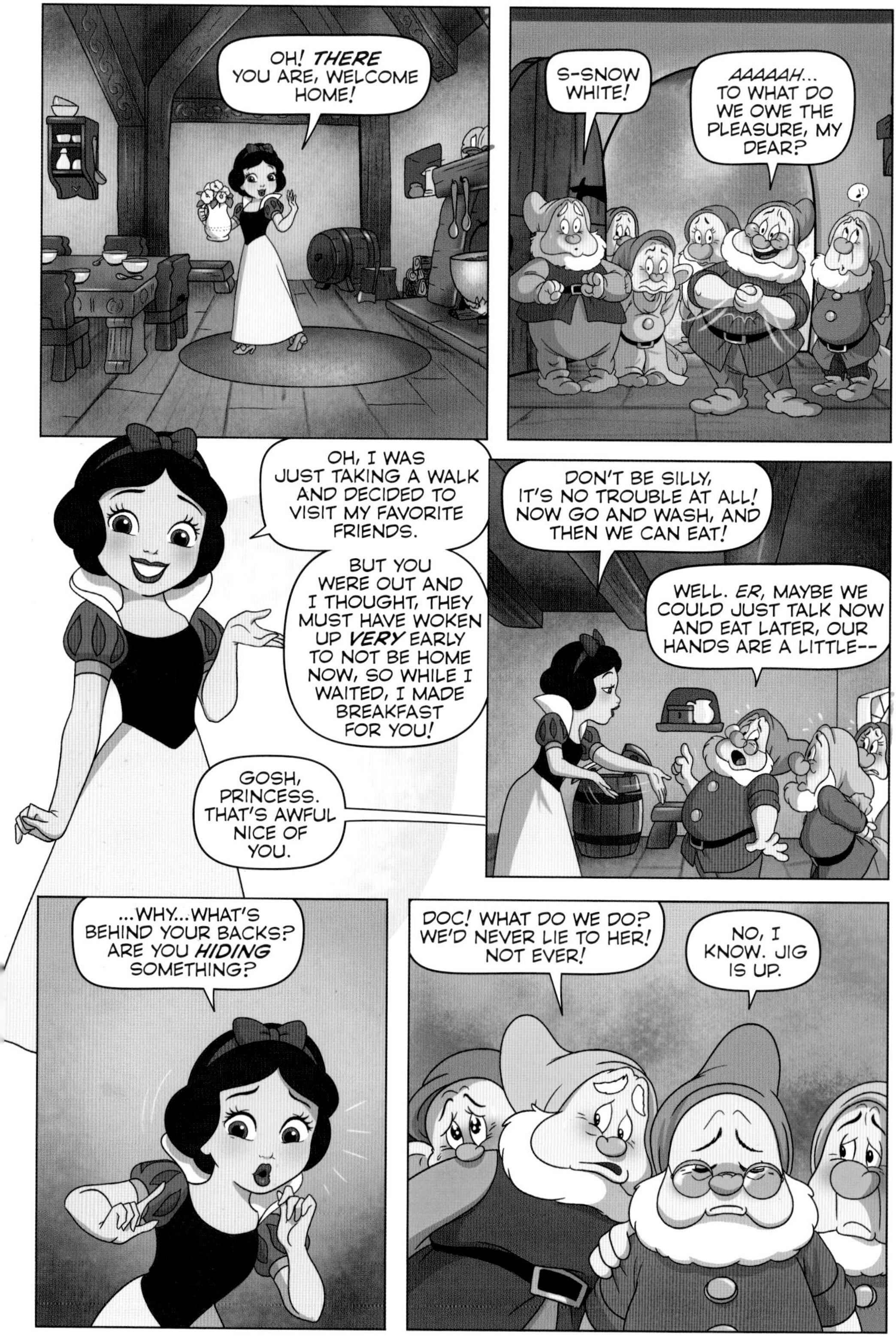
OH! THERE YOU ARE, WELCOME HOME!
S-SNOW WHITE!
AAAAAH... TO WHAT DO WE OWE THE PLEASURE, MY DEAR?
OH, I WAS JUST TAKING A WALK AND DECIDED TO VISIT MY FAVORITE FRIENDS.
BUT YOU WERE OUT AND I THOUGHT, THEY MUST HAVE WOKEN UP VERY EARLY TO NOT BE HOME NOW, SO WHILE I WAITED, I MADE BREAKFAST FOR YOU!
GOSH, PRINCESS. THAT'S AWFUL NICE OF YOU.
DON'T BE SILLY, IT'S NO TROUBLE AT ALL! NOW GO AND WASH, AND THEN WE CAN EAT!
WELL. ER, MAYBE WE COULD JUST TALK NOW AND EAT LATER, OUR HANDS ARE A LITTLE--
...WHY...WHAT'S BEHIND YOUR BACKS? ARE YOU HIDING SOMETHING?
DOC! WHAT DO WE DO? WE'D NEVER LIE TO HER! NOT EVER!
NO, I KNOW. JIG IS UP.

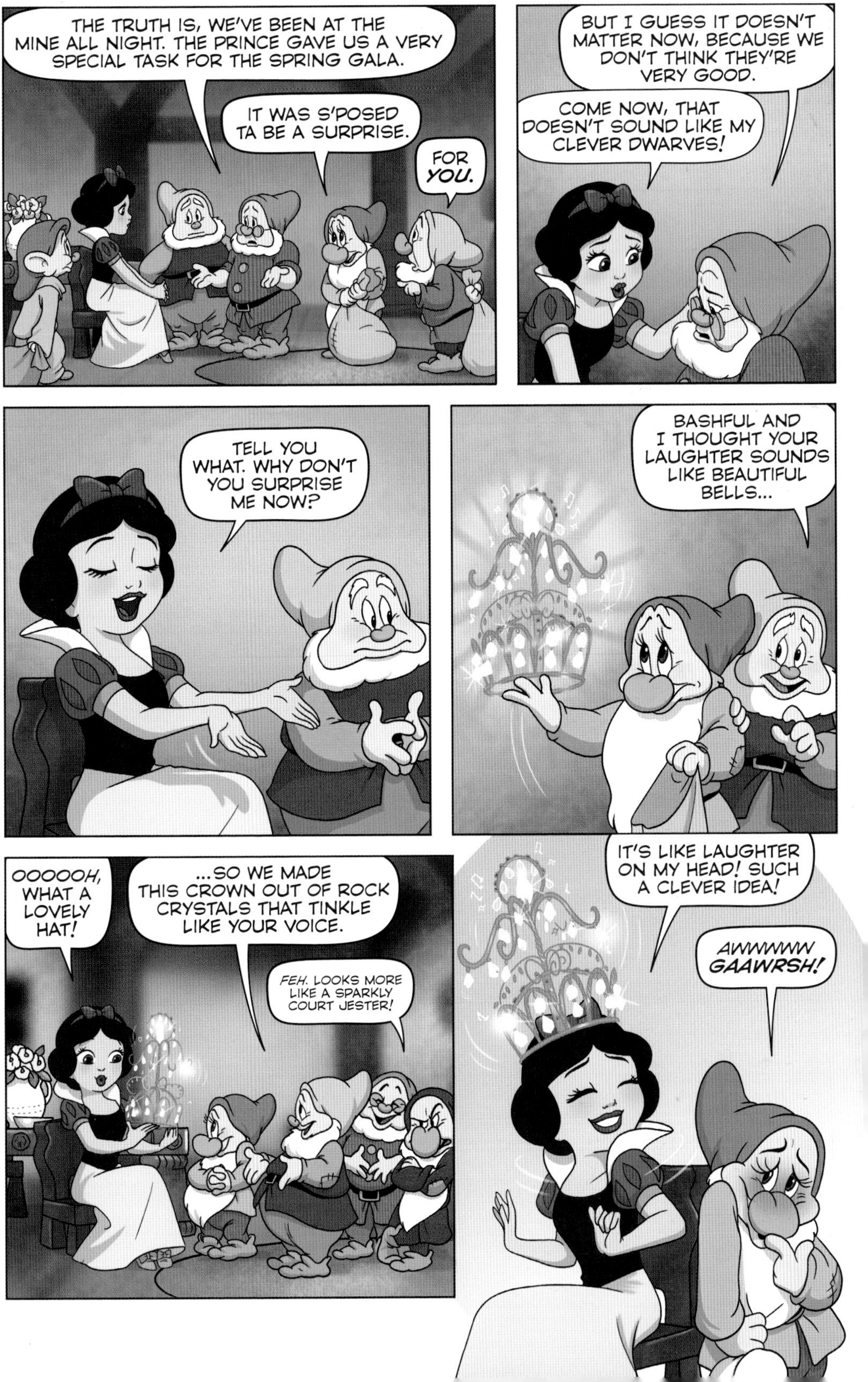
THE TRUTH IS, WE'VE BEEN AT THE MINE ALL NIGHT. THE PRINCE GAVE US A VERY SPECIAL TASK FOR THE SPRING GALA.
IT WAS S'POSED TA BE A SURPRISE.
FOR *YOU.*
BUT I GUESS IT DOESN'T MATTER NOW, BECAUSE WE DON'T THINK THEY'RE VERY GOOD.
COME NOW, THAT DOESN'T SOUND LIKE MY CLEVER DWARVES!
TELL YOU WHAT. WHY DON'T YOU SURPRISE ME NOW?
BASHFUL AND I THOUGHT YOUR LAUGHTER SOUNDS LIKE BEAUTIFUL BELLS...
OOOOOH, WHAT A LOVELY HAT!
...SO WE MADE THIS CROWN OUT OF ROCK CRYSTALS THAT TINKLE LIKE YOUR VOICE.
FEH. LOOKS MORE LIKE A SPARKLY COURT JESTER!
IT'S LIKE LAUGHTER ON MY HEAD! SUCH A CLEVER IDEA!
AWWWWWW GAAWRSH!

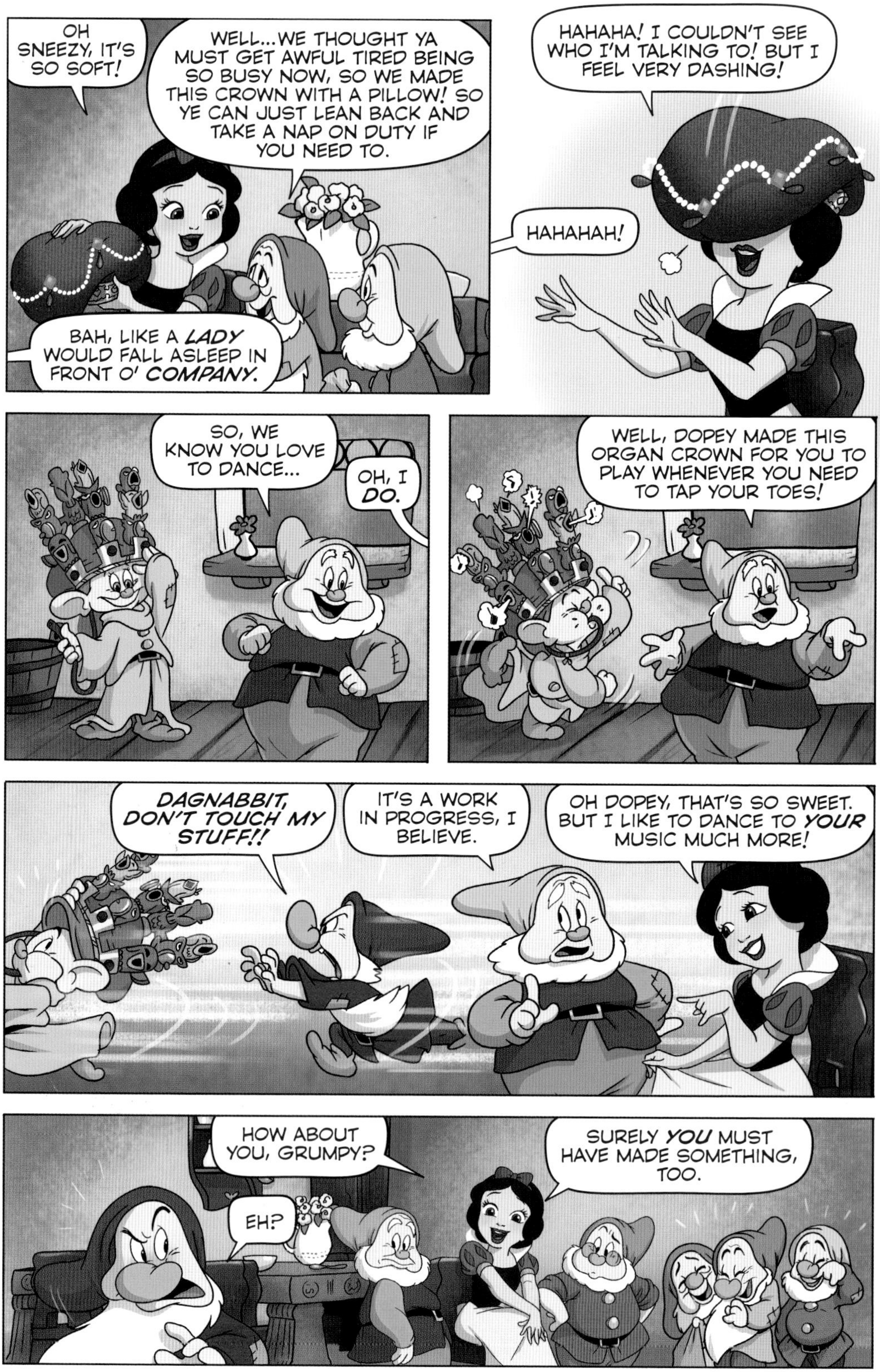
OH SNEEZY, IT'S SO SOFT!
WELL...WE THOUGHT YA MUST GET AWFUL TIRED BEING SO BUSY NOW, SO WE MADE THIS CROWN WITH A PILLOW! SO YE CAN JUST LEAN BACK AND TAKE A NAP ON DUTY IF YOU NEED TO.
BAH, LIKE A LADY WOULD FALL ASLEEP IN FRONT O' COMPANY.
HAHAHA! I COULDN'T SEE WHO I'M TALKING TO! BUT I FEEL VERY DASHING!
HAHAHAH!
SO, WE KNOW YOU LOVE TO DANCE...
OH, I DO.
WELL, DOPEY MADE THIS ORGAN CROWN FOR YOU TO PLAY WHENEVER YOU NEED TO TAP YOUR TOES!
DAGNABBIT, DON'T TOUCH MY STUFF!!
IT'S A WORK IN PROGRESS, I BELIEVE.
OH DOPEY, THAT'S SO SWEET. BUT I LIKE TO DANCE TO YOUR MUSIC MUCH MORE!
HOW ABOUT YOU, GRUMPY?
EH?
SURELY YOU MUST HAVE MADE SOMETHING, TOO.

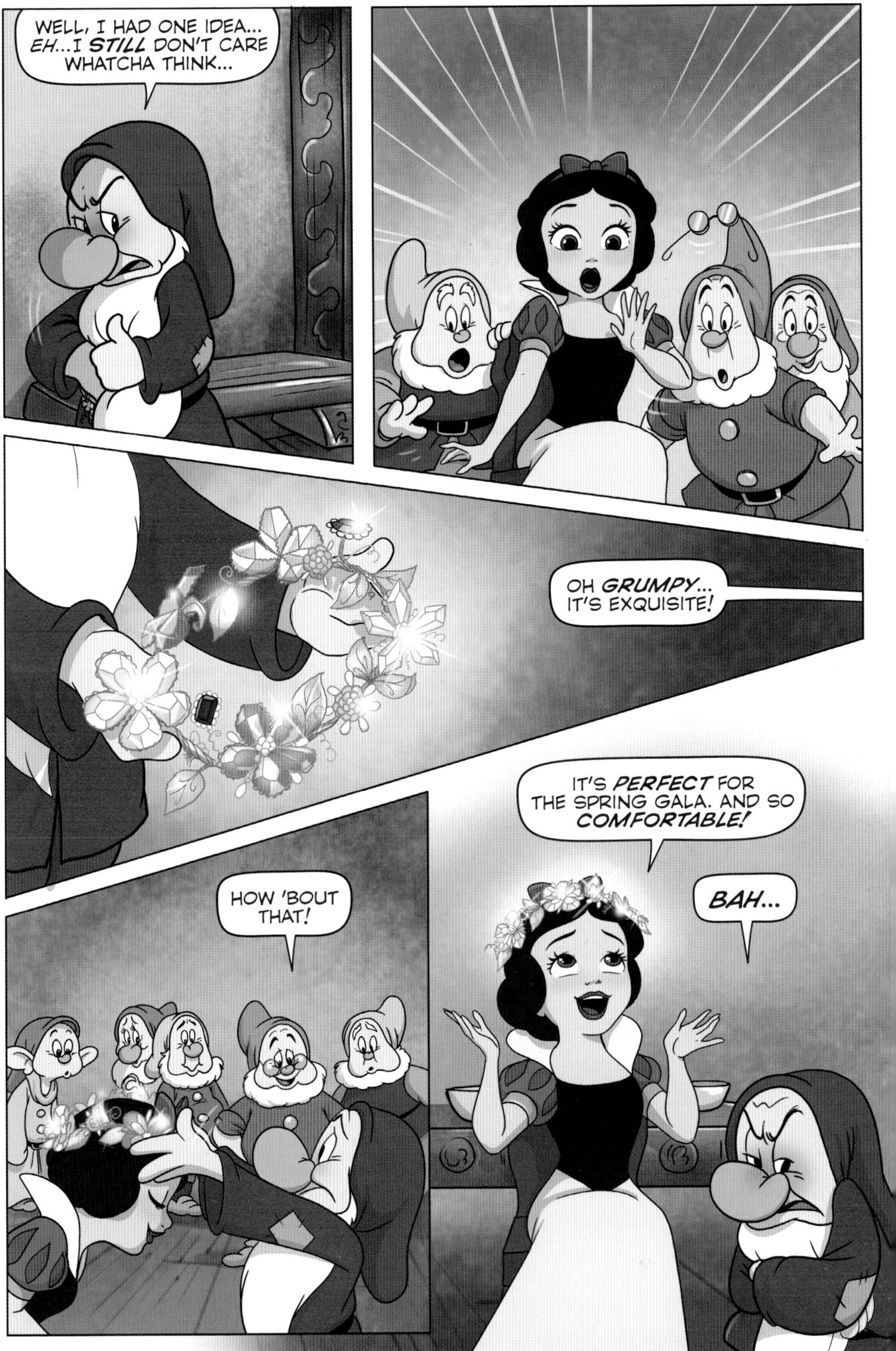
WELL, I HAD ONE IDEA... EH...I STILL DON'T CARE WHATCHA THINK...
OH GRUMPY... IT'S EXQUISITE!
HOW 'BOUT THAT!
IT'S PERFECT FOR THE SPRING GALA. AND SO COMFORTABLE!
BAH...

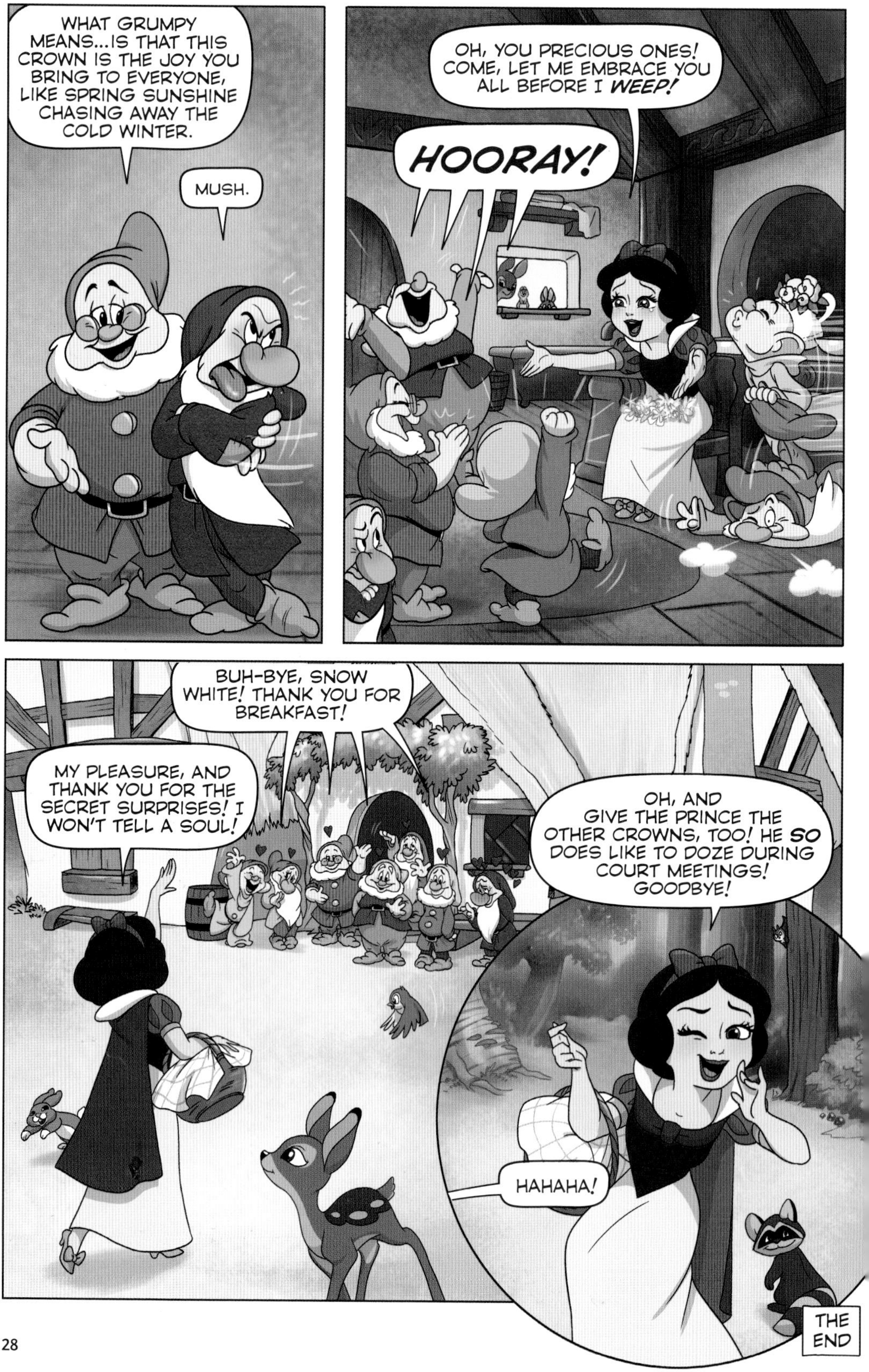
WHAT GRUMPY MEANS...IS THAT THIS CROWN IS THE JOY YOU BRING TO EVERYONE, LIKE SPRING SUNSHINE CHASING AWAY THE COLD WINTER.
MUSH.
OH, YOU PRECIOUS ONES! COME, LET ME EMBRACE YOU ALL BEFORE I *WEEP!*
HOORAY!
BUH-BYE, SNOW WHITE! THANK YOU FOR BREAKFAST!
MY PLEASURE, AND THANK YOU FOR THE SECRET SURPRISES! I WON'T TELL A SOUL!
OH, AND GIVE THE PRINCE THE OTHER CROWNS, TOO! HE **SO** DOES LIKE TO DOZE DURING COURT MEETINGS! GOODBYE!
HAHAHA!
THE END

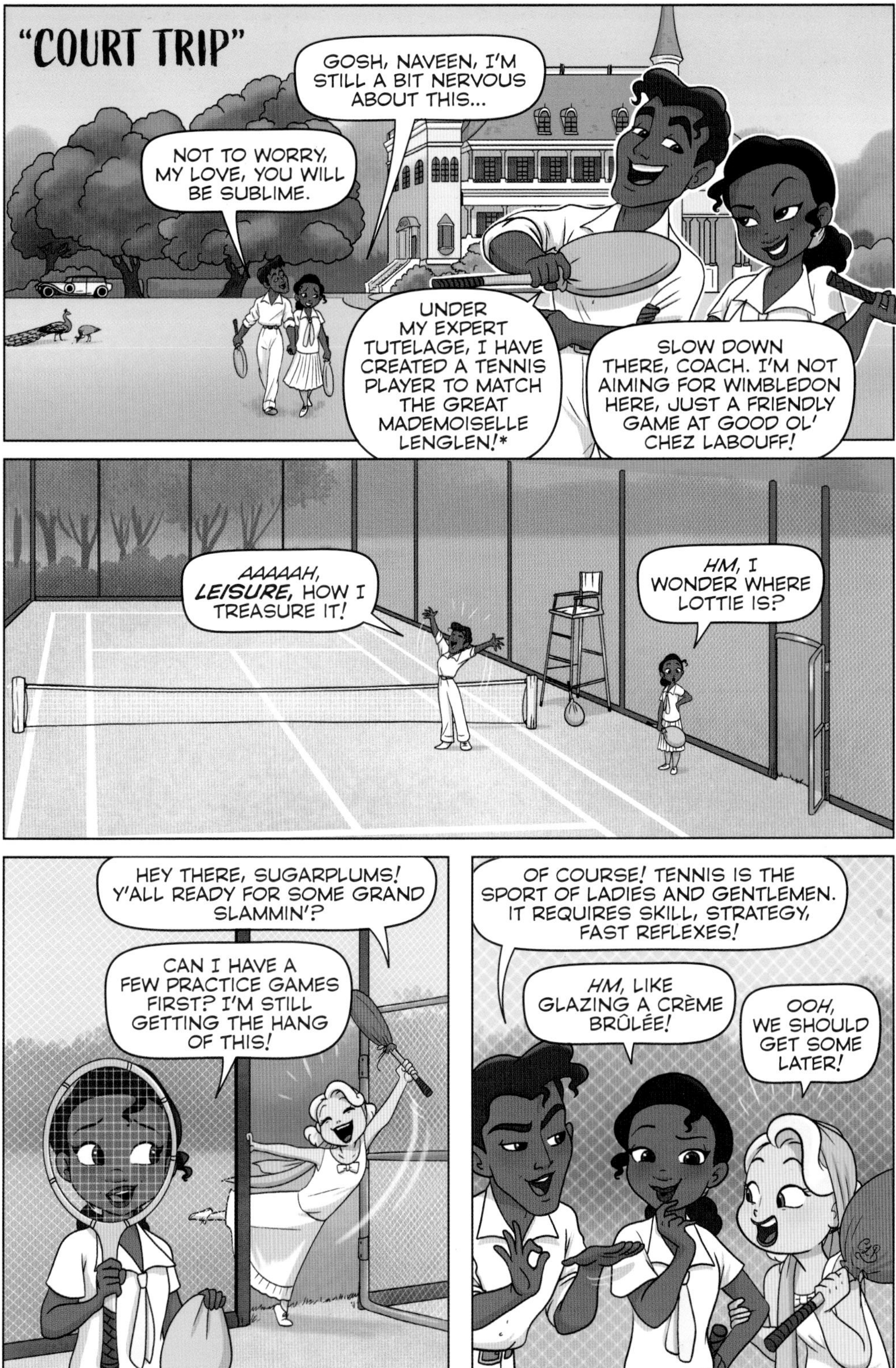
"COURT TRIP"
GOSH, NAVEEN, I'M STILL A BIT NERVOUS ABOUT THIS...
NOT TO WORRY, MY LOVE, YOU WILL BE SUBLIME.
UNDER MY EXPERT TUTELAGE, I HAVE CREATED A TENNIS PLAYER TO MATCH THE GREAT MADEMOISELLE LENGLEN!*
SLOW DOWN THERE, COACH. I'M NOT AIMING FOR WIMBLEDON HERE, JUST A FRIENDLY GAME AT GOOD OL' CHEZ LABOUFF!
AAAAAH, LEISURE, HOW I TREASURE IT!
HM, I WONDER WHERE LOTTIE IS?
HEY THERE, SUGARPLUMS! Y'ALL READY FOR SOME GRAND SLAMMIN'?
CAN I HAVE A FEW PRACTICE GAMES FIRST? I'M STILL GETTING THE HANG OF THIS!
OF COURSE! TENNIS IS THE SPORT OF LADIES AND GENTLEMEN. IT REQUIRES SKILL, STRATEGY, FAST REFLEXES!
HM, LIKE GLAZING A CRÈME BRÛLÉE!
OOH, WE SHOULD GET SOME LATER!

*SUZANNE LENGLEN WAS THE #1 WOMEN'S SEED AT WIMBLEDON FOR MOST OF THE 1920S.

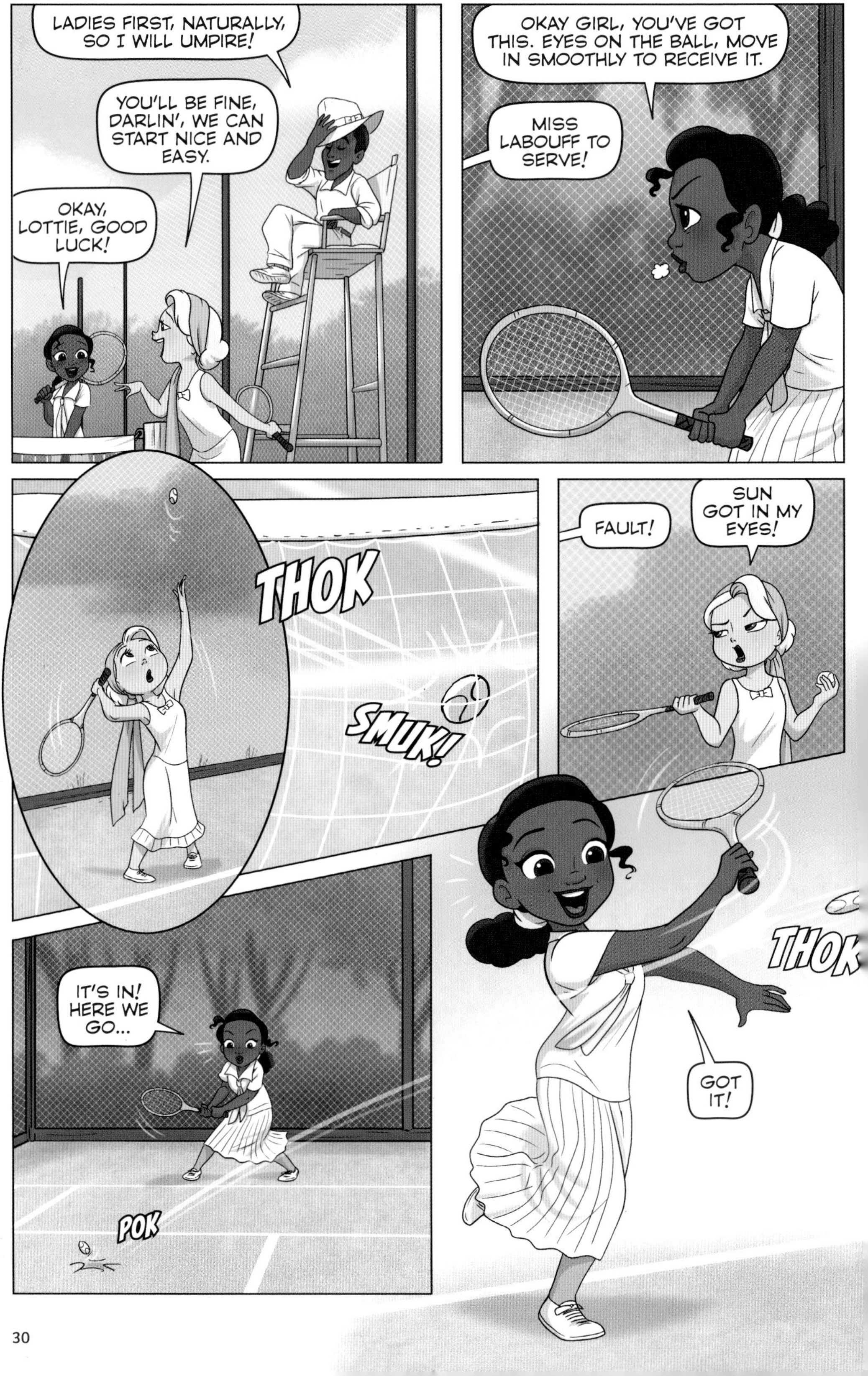
LADIES FIRST, NATURALLY, SO I WILL UMPIRE!
YOU'LL BE FINE, DARLIN', WE CAN START NICE AND EASY.
OKAY, LOTTIE, GOOD LUCK!
OKAY GIRL, YOU'VE GOT THIS. EYES ON THE BALL, MOVE IN SMOOTHLY TO RECEIVE IT.
MISS LABOUFF TO SERVE!
THOK
SMUK!
FAULT!
SUN GOT IN MY EYES!
IT'S IN! HERE WE GO...
POK
THOK
GOT IT!

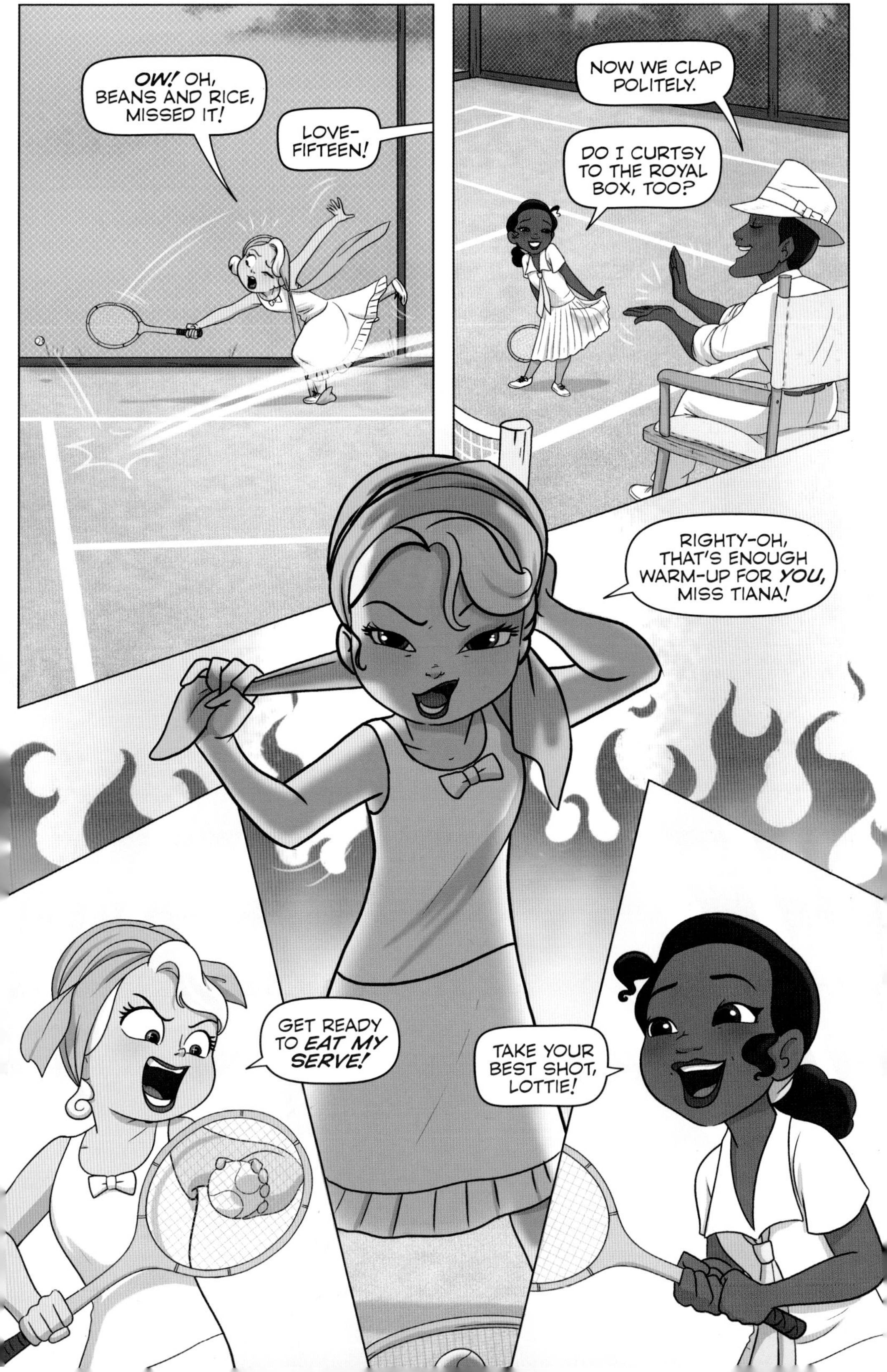
OW! OH, BEANS AND RICE, MISSED IT!
LOVE-FIFTEEN!
NOW WE CLAP POLITELY.
DO I CURTSY TO THE ROYAL BOX, TOO?
RIGHTY-OH, THAT'S ENOUGH WARM-UP FOR YOU, MISS TIANA!
GET READY TO EAT MY SERVE!
TAKE YOUR BEST SHOT, LOTTIE!

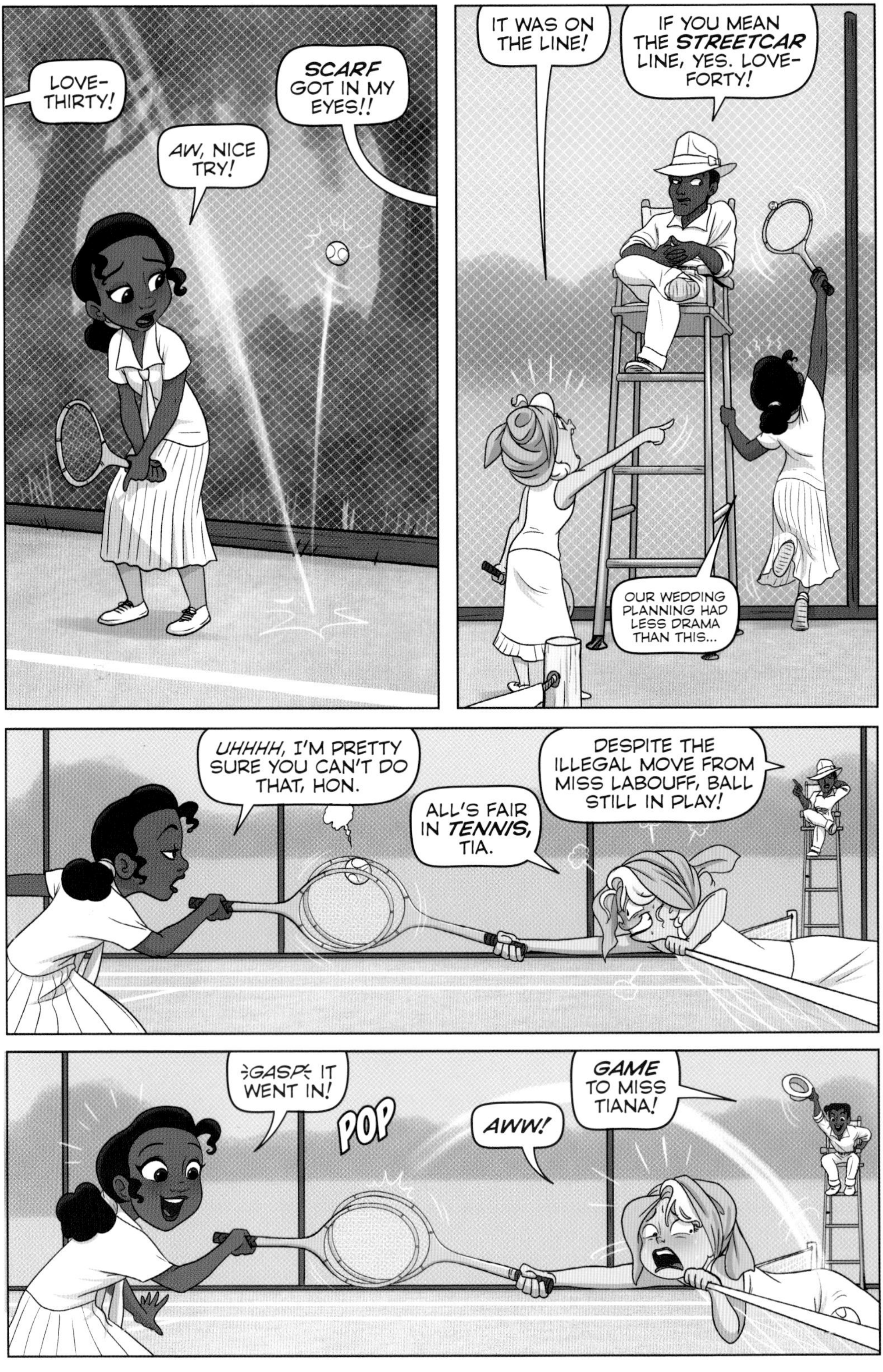
LOVE-THIRTY!
SCARF GOT IN MY EYES!!
AW, NICE TRY!
IT WAS ON THE LINE!
IF YOU MEAN THE STREETCAR LINE, YES. LOVE-FORTY!
OUR WEDDING PLANNING HAD LESS DRAMA THAN THIS...
UHHHH, I'M PRETTY SURE YOU CAN'T DO THAT, HON.
ALL'S FAIR IN TENNIS, TIA.
DESPITE THE ILLEGAL MOVE FROM MISS LABOUFF, BALL STILL IN PLAY!
GASP IT WENT IN!
POP
AWW!
GAME TO MISS TIANA!

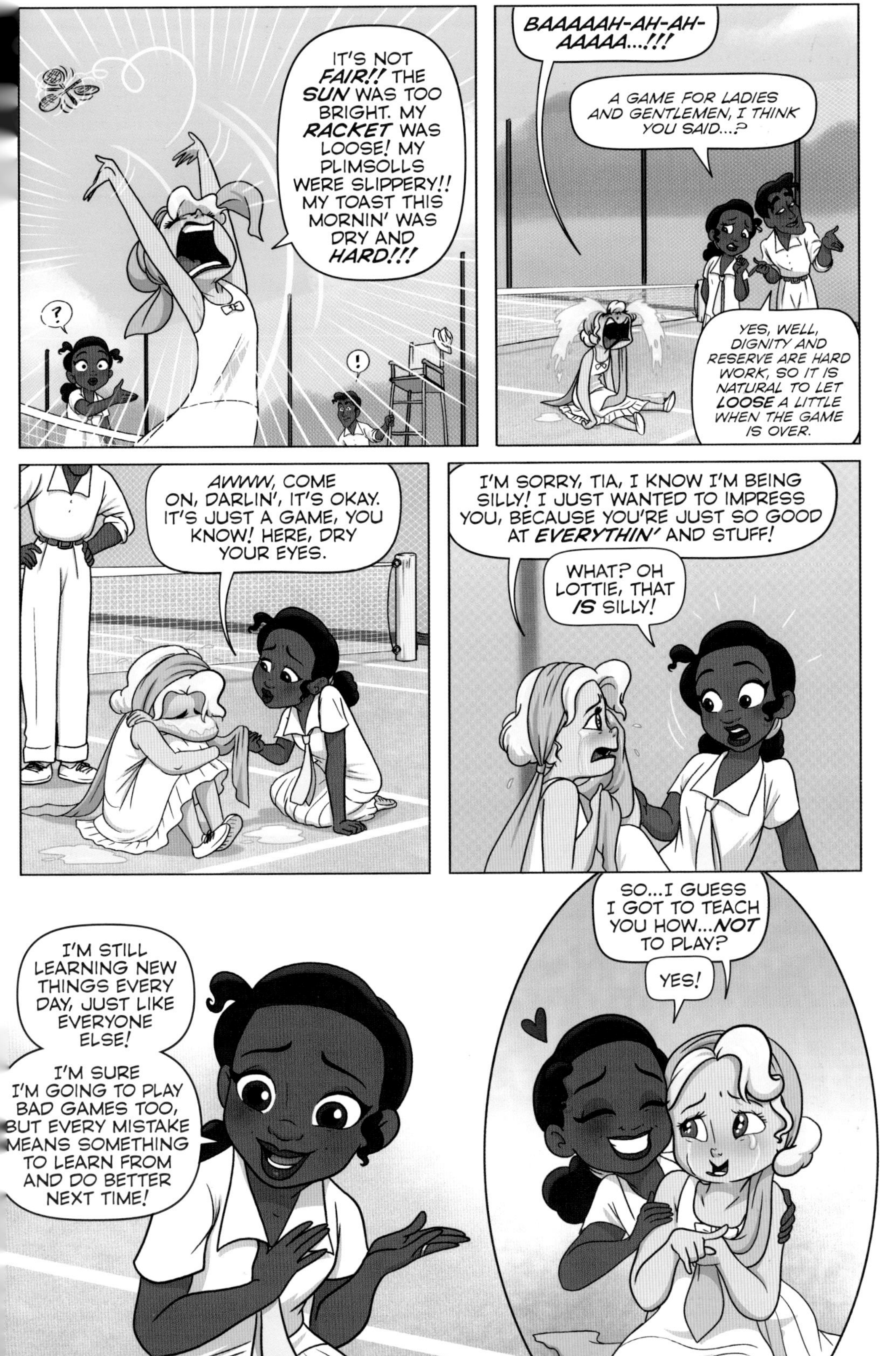
IT'S NOT FAIR!! THE SUN WAS TOO BRIGHT. MY RACKET WAS LOOSE! MY PLIMSOLLS WERE SLIPPERY!! MY TOAST THIS MORNIN' WAS DRY AND HARD!!!
?
!
BAAAAAH-AH-AH-AAAAA...!!!
A GAME FOR LADIES AND GENTLEMEN, I THINK YOU SAID...?
YES, WELL, DIGNITY AND RESERVE ARE HARD WORK, SO IT IS NATURAL TO LET LOOSE A LITTLE WHEN THE GAME IS OVER.
AWWW, COME ON, DARLIN', IT'S OKAY. IT'S JUST A GAME, YOU KNOW! HERE, DRY YOUR EYES.
I'M SORRY, TIA, I KNOW I'M BEING SILLY! I JUST WANTED TO IMPRESS YOU, BECAUSE YOU'RE JUST SO GOOD AT EVERYTHIN' AND STUFF!
WHAT? OH LOTTIE, THAT IS SILLY!
I'M STILL LEARNING NEW THINGS EVERY DAY, JUST LIKE EVERYONE ELSE!
I'M SURE I'M GOING TO PLAY BAD GAMES TOO, BUT EVERY MISTAKE MEANS SOMETHING TO LEARN FROM AND DO BETTER NEXT TIME!
SO...I GUESS I GOT TO TEACH YOU HOW...NOT TO PLAY?
YES!

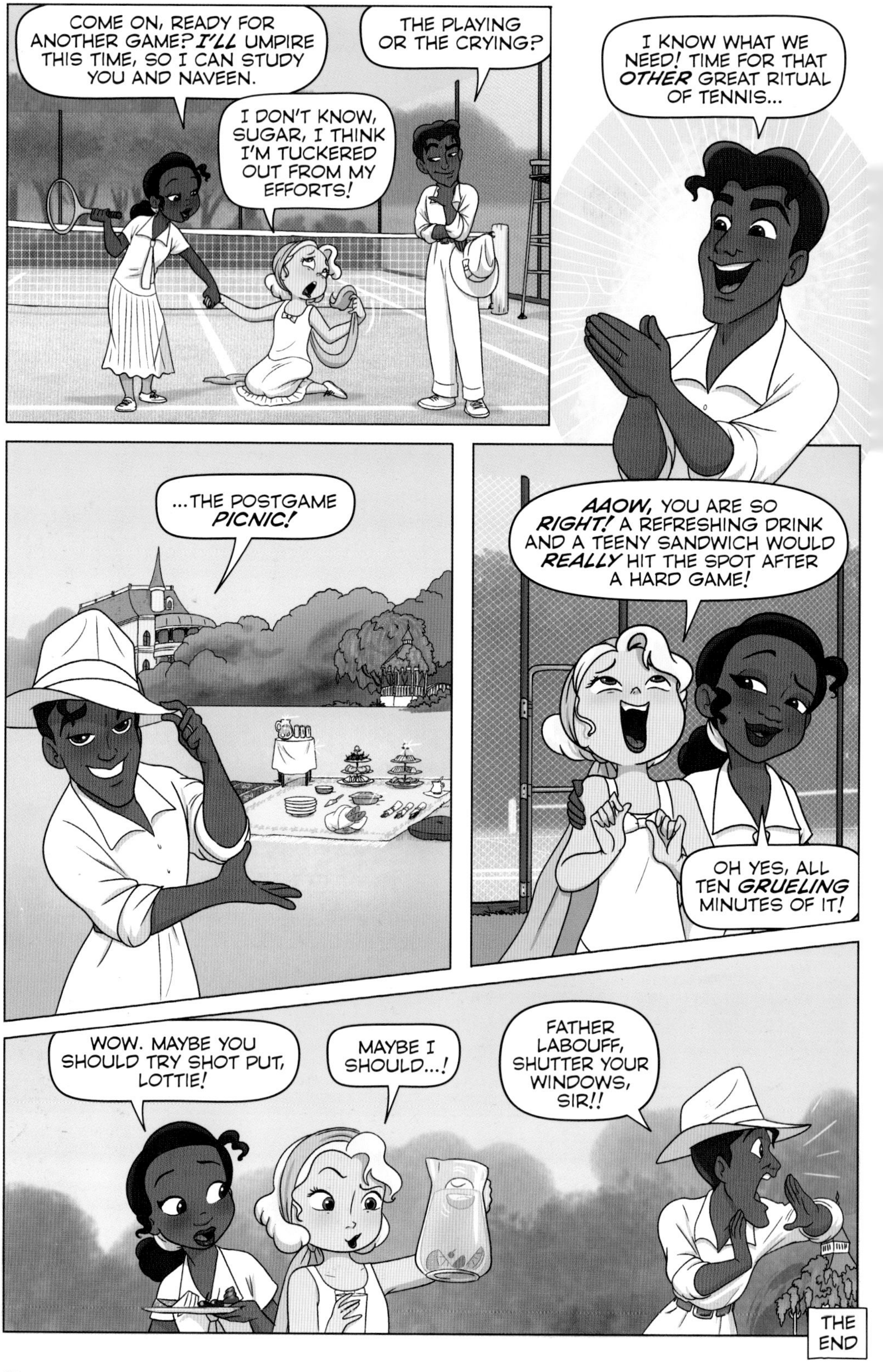
COME ON, READY FOR ANOTHER GAME? I'LL UMPIRE THIS TIME, SO I CAN STUDY YOU AND NAVEEN.
THE PLAYING OR THE CRYING?
I DON'T KNOW, SUGAR, I THINK I'M TUCKERED OUT FROM MY EFFORTS!
I KNOW WHAT WE NEED! TIME FOR THAT OTHER GREAT RITUAL OF TENNIS...
...THE POSTGAME PICNIC!
AAOW, YOU ARE SO RIGHT! A REFRESHING DRINK AND A TEENY SANDWICH WOULD REALLY HIT THE SPOT AFTER A HARD GAME!
OH YES, ALL TEN GRUELING MINUTES OF IT!
WOW. MAYBE YOU SHOULD TRY SHOT PUT, LOTTIE!
MAYBE I SHOULD...!
FATHER LABOUFF, SHUTTER YOUR WINDOWS, SIR!!
THE END

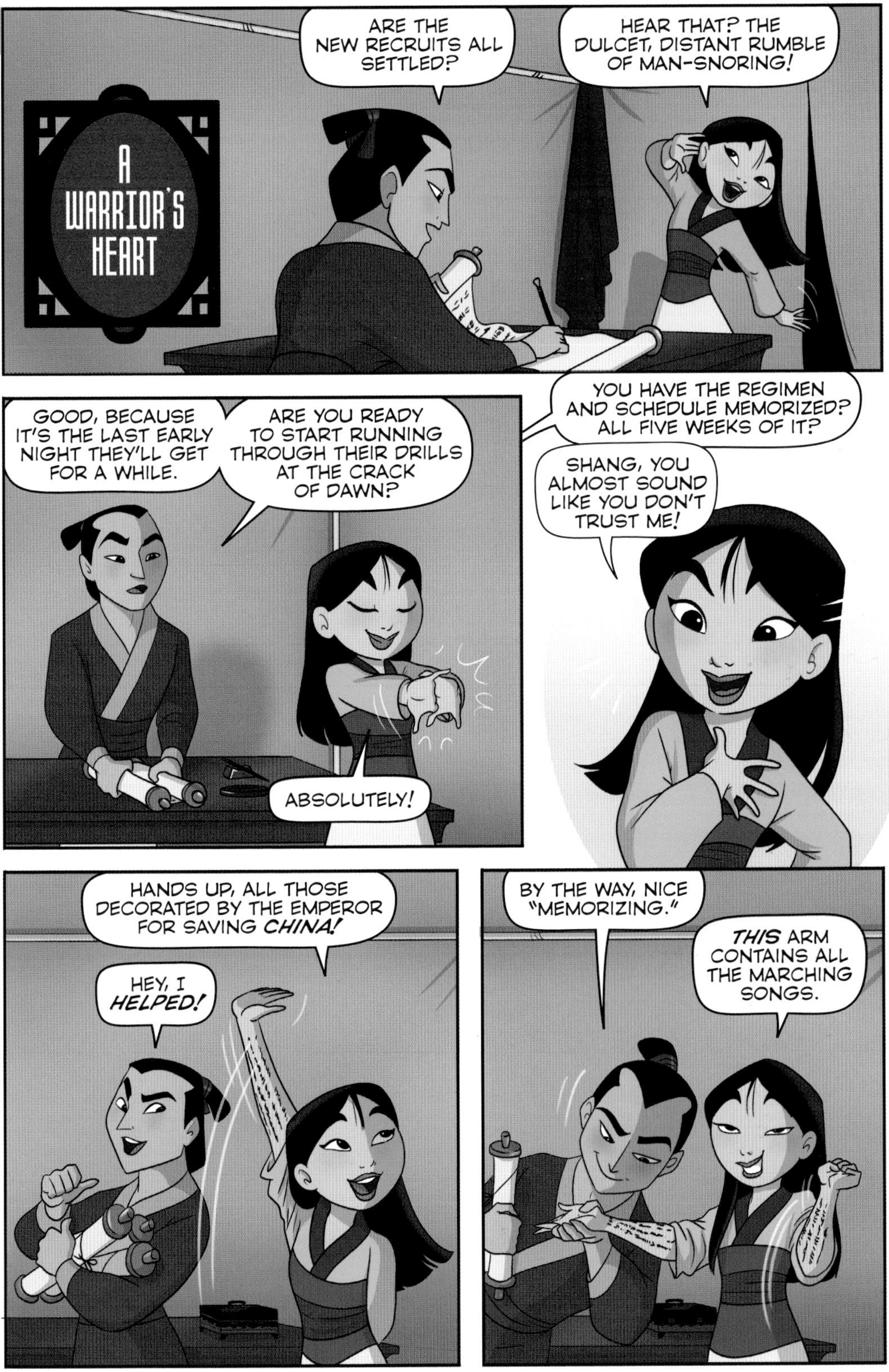
A WARRIOR'S HEART
ARE THE NEW RECRUITS ALL SETTLED?
HEAR THAT? THE DULCET, DISTANT RUMBLE OF MAN-SNORING!
GOOD, BECAUSE IT'S THE LAST EARLY NIGHT THEY'LL GET FOR A WHILE.
ARE YOU READY TO START RUNNING THROUGH THEIR DRILLS AT THE CRACK OF DAWN?
ABSOLUTELY!
YOU HAVE THE REGIMEN AND SCHEDULE MEMORIZED? ALL FIVE WEEKS OF IT?
SHANG, YOU ALMOST SOUND LIKE YOU DON'T TRUST ME!
HANDS UP, ALL THOSE DECORATED BY THE EMPEROR FOR SAVING *CHINA!*
HEY, I *HELPED!*
BY THE WAY, NICE "MEMORIZING."
THIS ARM CONTAINS ALL THE MARCHING SONGS.

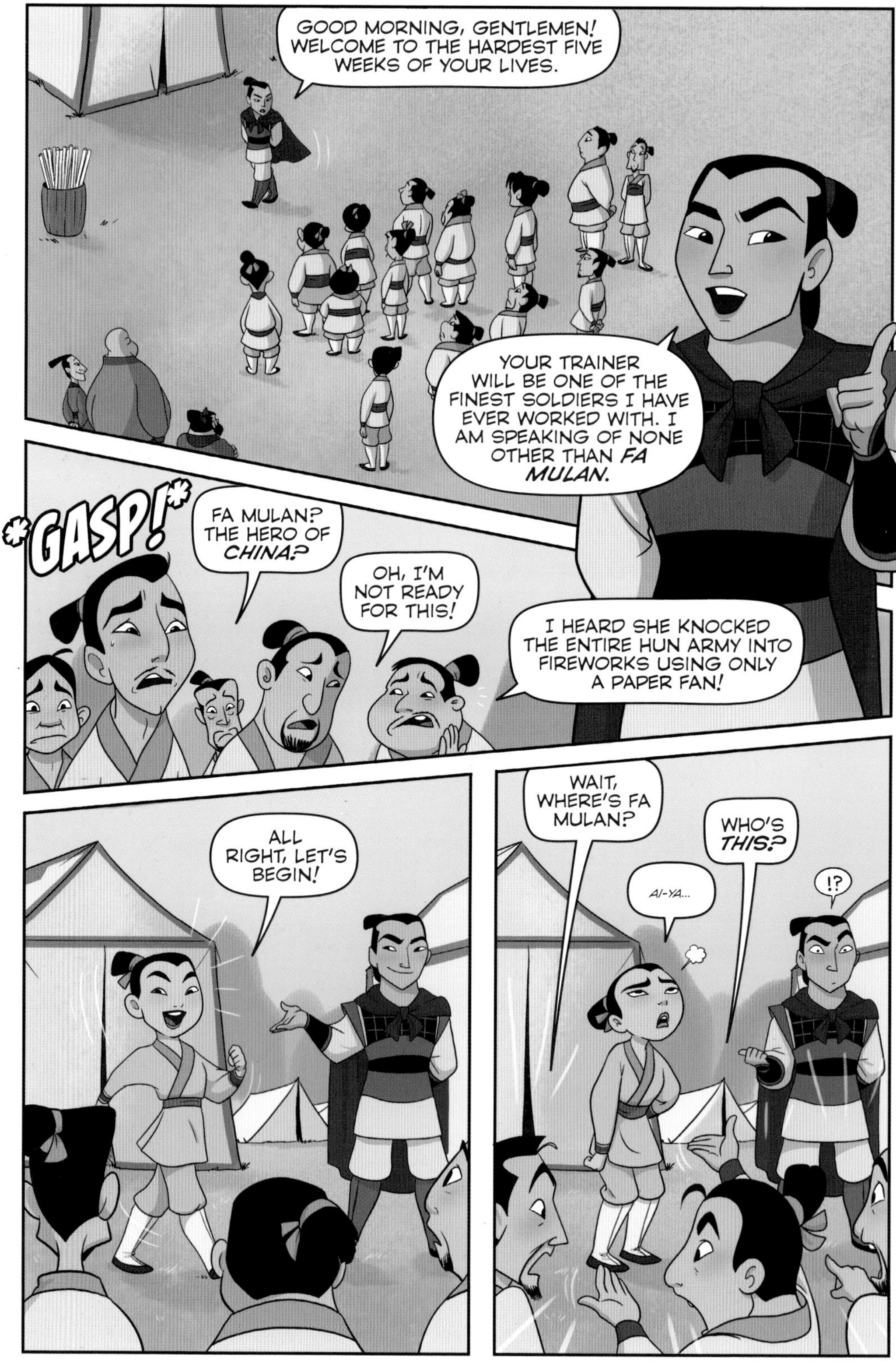
GOOD MORNING, GENTLEMEN! WELCOME TO THE HARDEST FIVE WEEKS OF YOUR LIVES.
YOUR TRAINER WILL BE ONE OF THE FINEST SOLDIERS I HAVE EVER WORKED WITH. I AM SPEAKING OF NONE OTHER THAN FA MULAN.
GASP!
FA MULAN? THE HERO OF CHINA?
OH, I'M NOT READY FOR THIS!
I HEARD SHE KNOCKED THE ENTIRE HUN ARMY INTO FIREWORKS USING ONLY A PAPER FAN!
ALL RIGHT, LET'S BEGIN!
WAIT, WHERE'S FA MULAN?
AI-YA...
WHO'S THIS?
!?

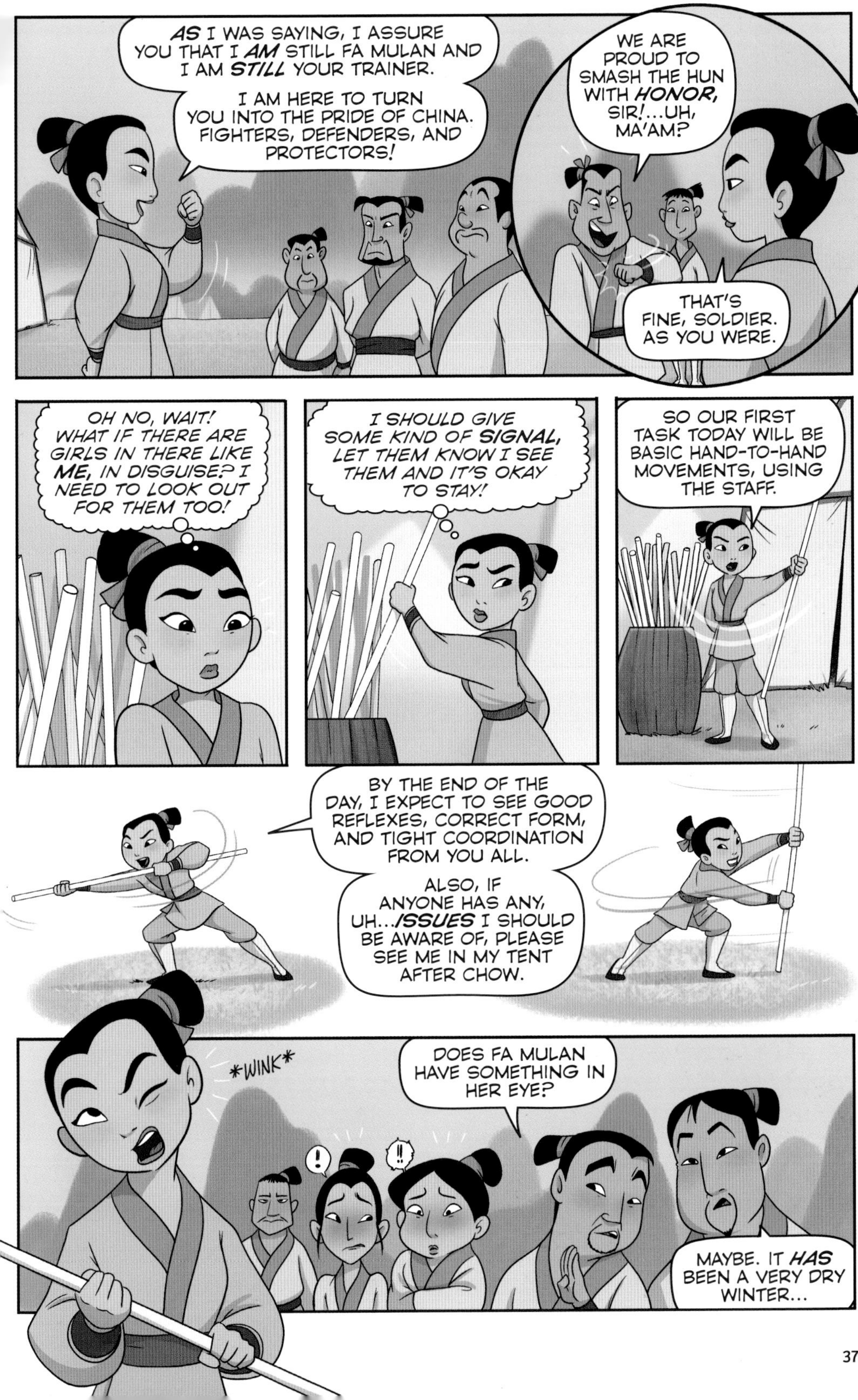
AS I WAS SAYING, I ASSURE YOU THAT I AM STILL FA MULAN AND I AM STILL YOUR TRAINER.
I AM HERE TO TURN YOU INTO THE PRIDE OF CHINA. FIGHTERS, DEFENDERS, AND PROTECTORS!
WE ARE PROUD TO SMASH THE HUN WITH HONOR, SIR!...UH, MA'AM?
THAT'S FINE, SOLDIER. AS YOU WERE.
OH NO, WAIT! WHAT IF THERE ARE GIRLS IN THERE LIKE ME, IN DISGUISE? I NEED TO LOOK OUT FOR THEM TOO!
I SHOULD GIVE SOME KIND OF SIGNAL, LET THEM KNOW I SEE THEM AND IT'S OKAY TO STAY!
SO OUR FIRST TASK TODAY WILL BE BASIC HAND-TO-HAND MOVEMENTS, USING THE STAFF.
BY THE END OF THE DAY, I EXPECT TO SEE GOOD REFLEXES, CORRECT FORM, AND TIGHT COORDINATION FROM YOU ALL.
ALSO, IF ANYONE HAS ANY, UH...ISSUES I SHOULD BE AWARE OF, PLEASE SEE ME IN MY TENT AFTER CHOW.
WINK
DOES FA MULAN HAVE SOMETHING IN HER EYE?
!
!!
MAYBE. IT HAS BEEN A VERY DRY WINTER...

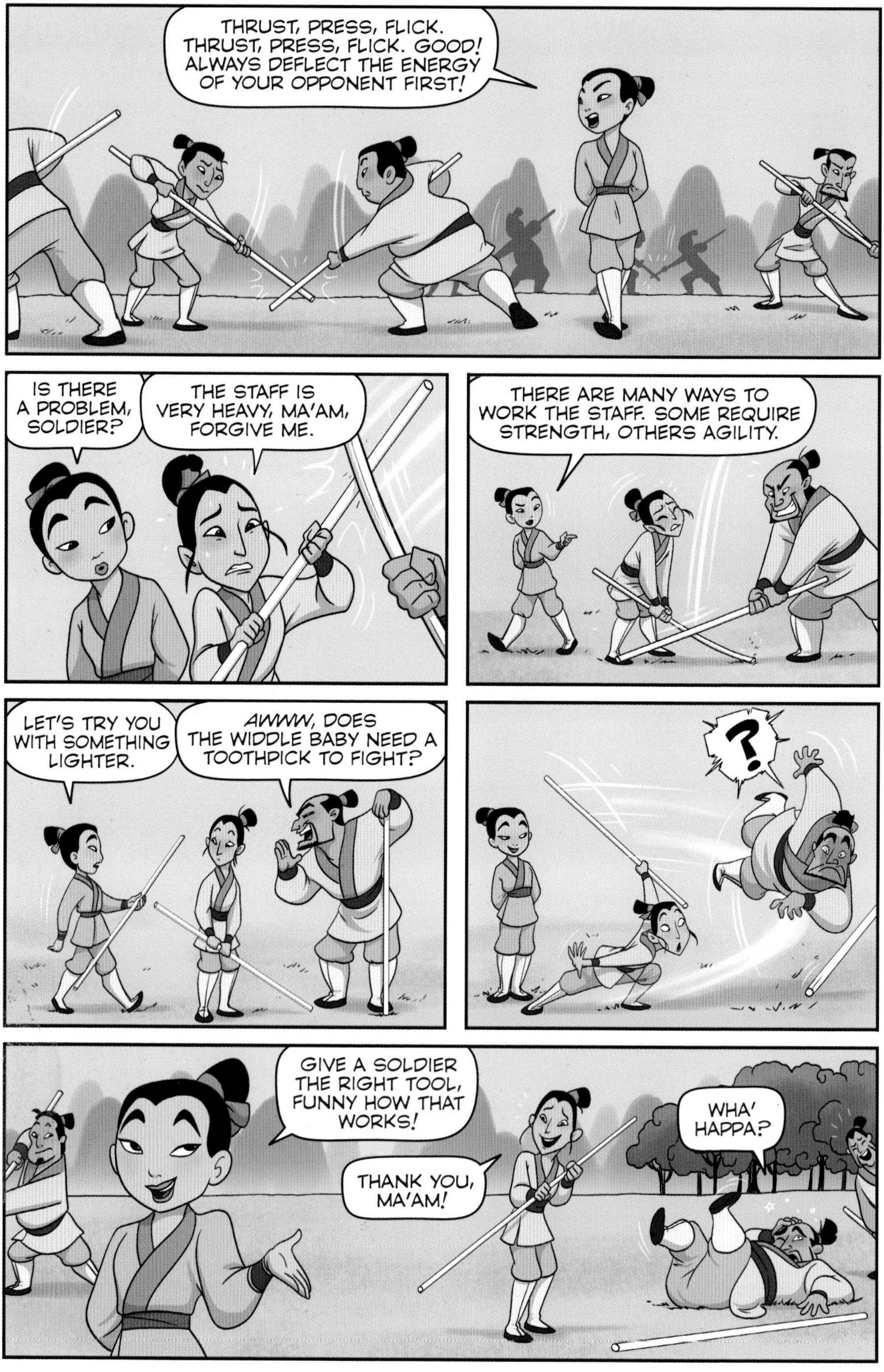
THRUST, PRESS, FLICK. THRUST, PRESS, FLICK. GOOD! ALWAYS DEFLECT THE ENERGY OF YOUR OPPONENT FIRST!
IS THERE A PROBLEM, SOLDIER?
THE STAFF IS VERY HEAVY, MA'AM, FORGIVE ME.
THERE ARE MANY WAYS TO WORK THE STAFF. SOME REQUIRE STRENGTH, OTHERS AGILITY.
LET'S TRY YOU WITH SOMETHING LIGHTER.
AWWW, DOES THE WIDDLE BABY NEED A TOOTHPICK TO FIGHT?
?
GIVE A SOLDIER THE RIGHT TOOL, FUNNY HOW THAT WORKS!
THANK YOU, MA'AM!
WHA' HAPPA?

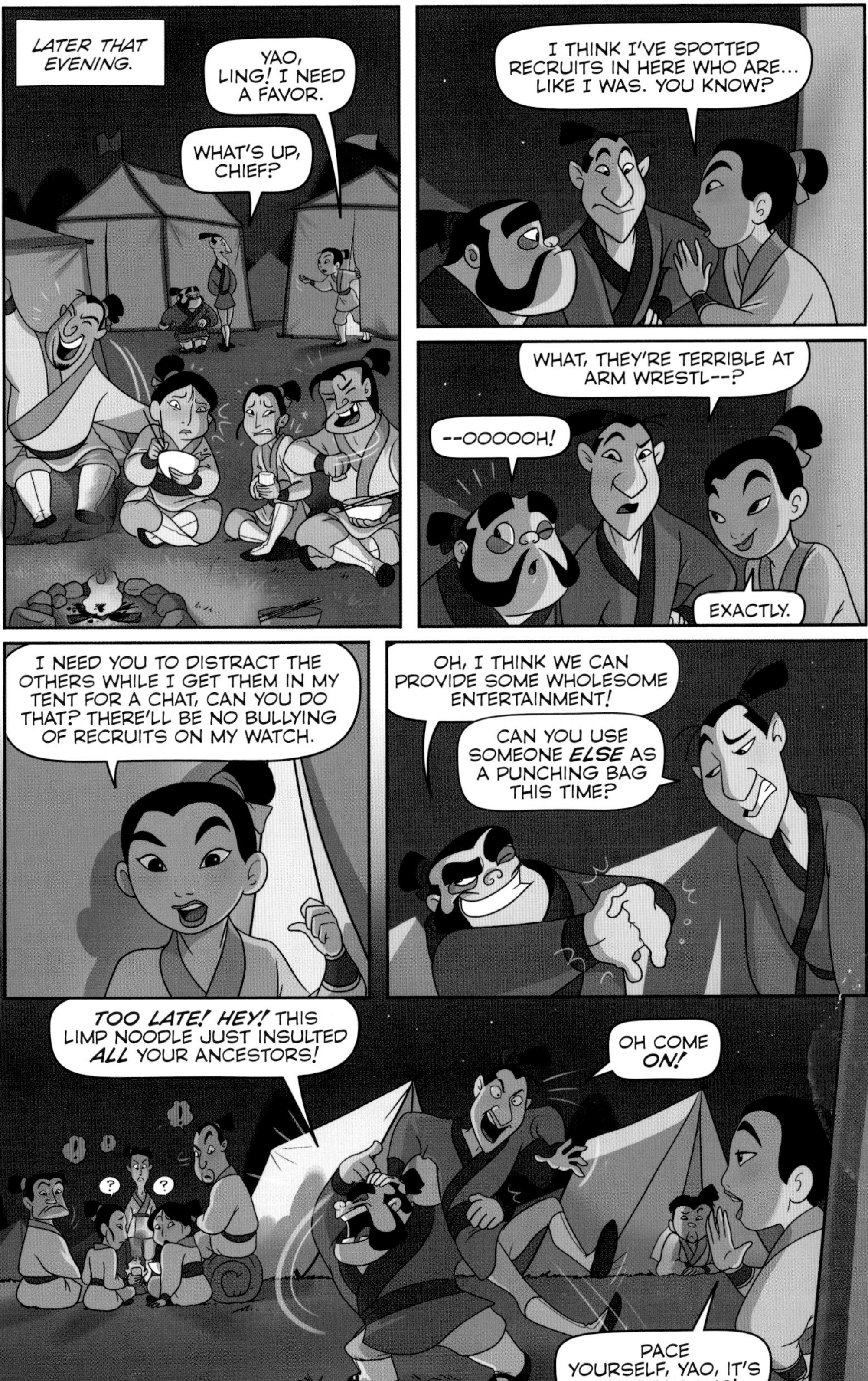
LATER THAT EVENING.
YAO, LING! I NEED A FAVOR.
WHAT'S UP, CHIEF?
I THINK I'VE SPOTTED RECRUITS IN HERE WHO ARE... LIKE I WAS. YOU KNOW?
WHAT, THEY'RE TERRIBLE AT ARM WRESTL--?
--OOOOOH!
EXACTLY.
I NEED YOU TO DISTRACT THE OTHERS WHILE I GET THEM IN MY TENT FOR A CHAT, CAN YOU DO THAT? THERE'LL BE NO BULLYING OF RECRUITS ON MY WATCH.
OH, I THINK WE CAN PROVIDE SOME WHOLESOME ENTERTAINMENT!
CAN YOU USE SOMEONE ELSE AS A PUNCHING BAG THIS TIME?
TOO LATE! HEY! THIS LIMP NOODLE JUST INSULTED ALL YOUR ANCESTORS!
OH COME ON!
PACE YOURSELF, YAO, IT'S ONLY DAY ONE!

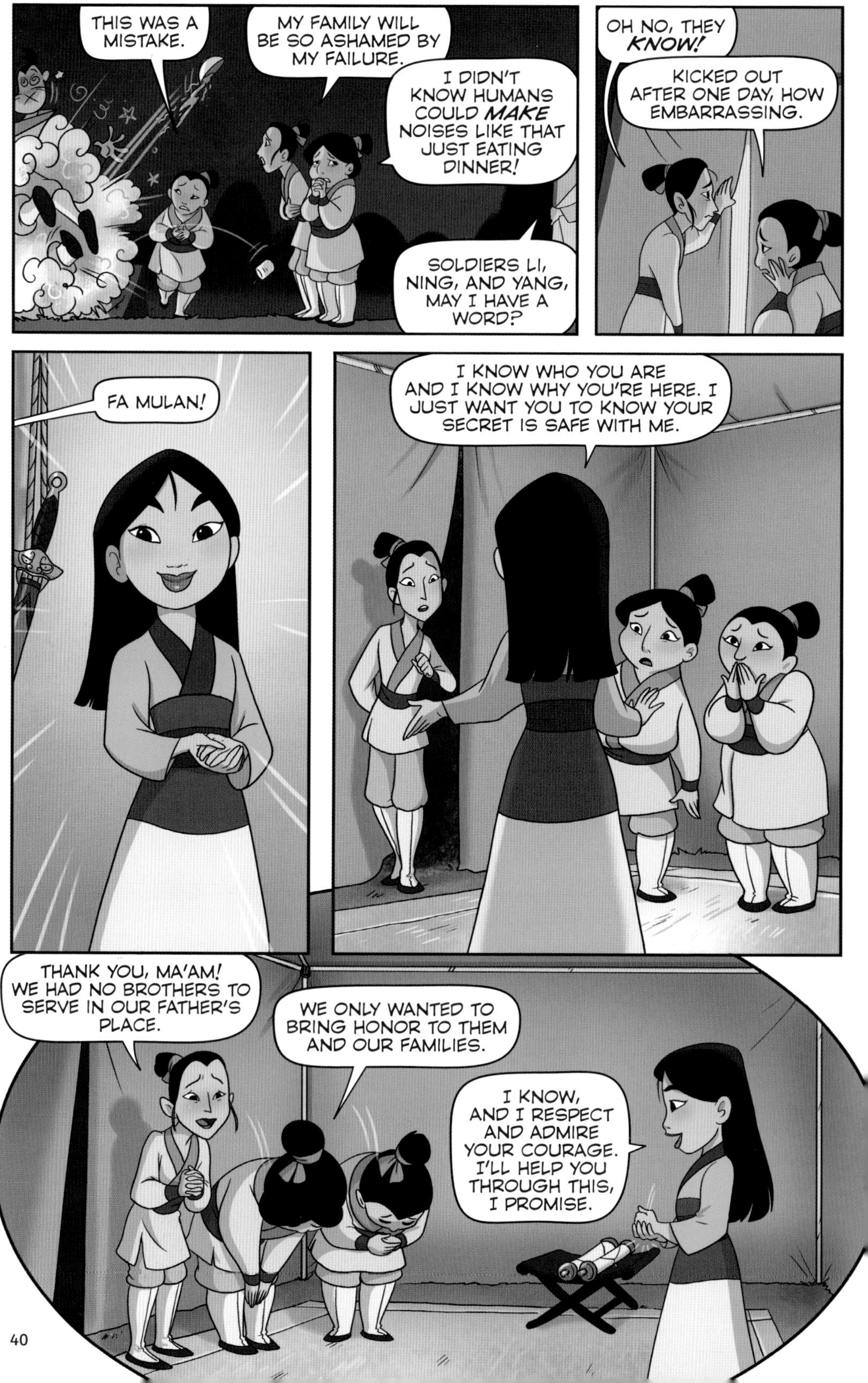

THIS WAS A MISTAKE.
MY FAMILY WILL BE SO ASHAMED BY MY FAILURE.
I DIDN'T KNOW HUMANS COULD *MAKE* NOISES LIKE THAT JUST EATING DINNER!
SOLDIERS LI, NING, AND YANG, MAY I HAVE A WORD?
OH NO, THEY *KNOW!*
KICKED OUT AFTER ONE DAY, HOW EMBARRASSING.
FA MULAN!
I KNOW WHO YOU ARE AND I KNOW WHY YOU'RE HERE. I JUST WANT YOU TO KNOW YOUR SECRET IS SAFE WITH ME.
THANK YOU, MA'AM! WE HAD NO BROTHERS TO SERVE IN OUR FATHER'S PLACE.
WE ONLY WANTED TO BRING HONOR TO THEM AND OUR FAMILIES.
I KNOW, AND I RESPECT AND ADMIRE YOUR COURAGE. I'LL HELP YOU THROUGH THIS, I PROMISE.

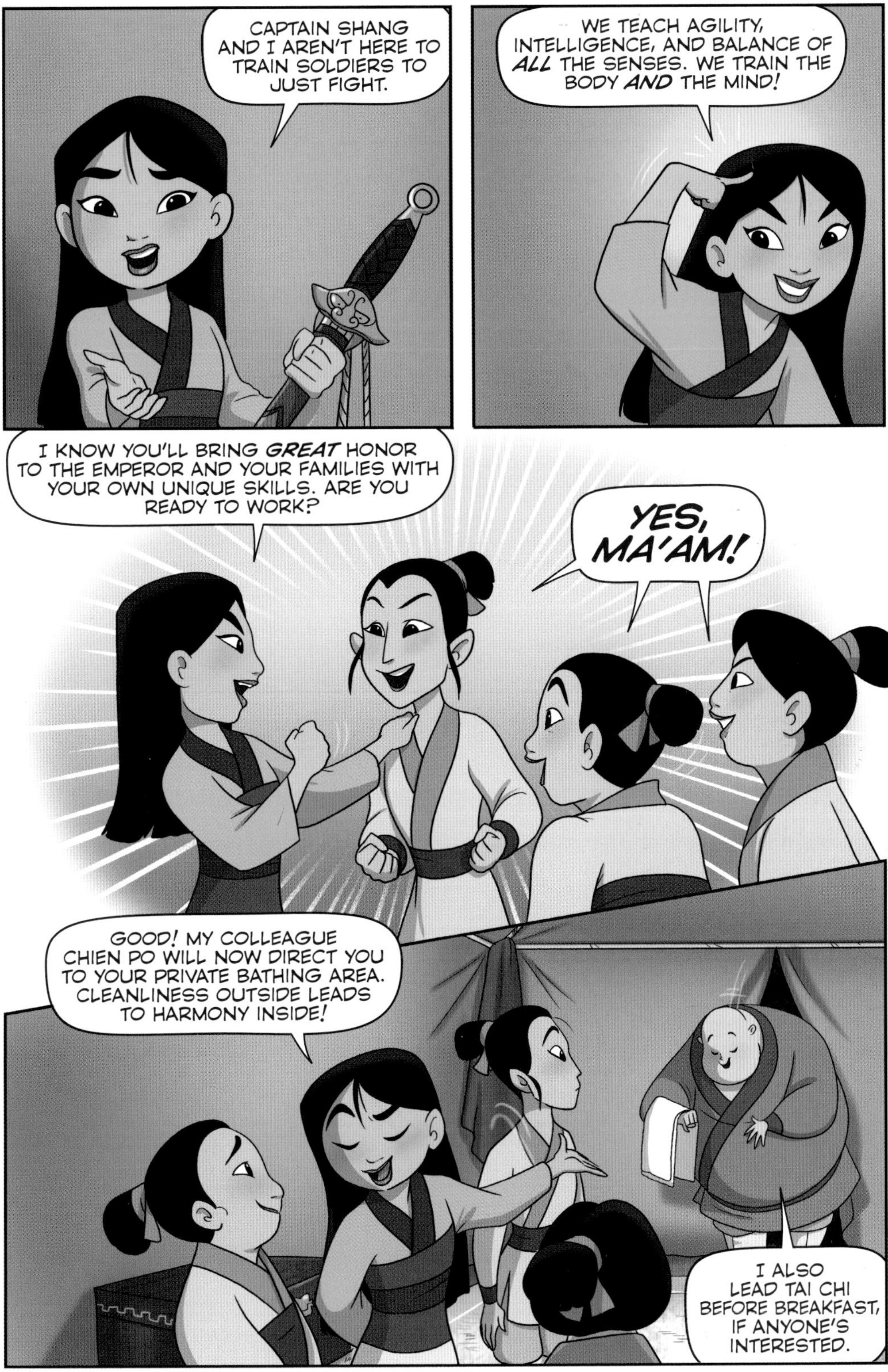
CAPTAIN SHANG AND I AREN'T HERE TO TRAIN SOLDIERS TO JUST FIGHT.
WE TEACH AGILITY, INTELLIGENCE, AND BALANCE OF *ALL* THE SENSES. WE TRAIN THE BODY *AND* THE MIND!
I KNOW YOU'LL BRING *GREAT* HONOR TO THE EMPEROR AND YOUR FAMILIES WITH YOUR OWN UNIQUE SKILLS. ARE YOU READY TO WORK?
YES, MA'AM!
GOOD! MY COLLEAGUE CHIEN PO WILL NOW DIRECT YOU TO YOUR PRIVATE BATHING AREA. CLEANLINESS OUTSIDE LEADS TO HARMONY INSIDE!
I ALSO LEAD TAI CHI BEFORE BREAKFAST, IF ANYONE'S INTERESTED.

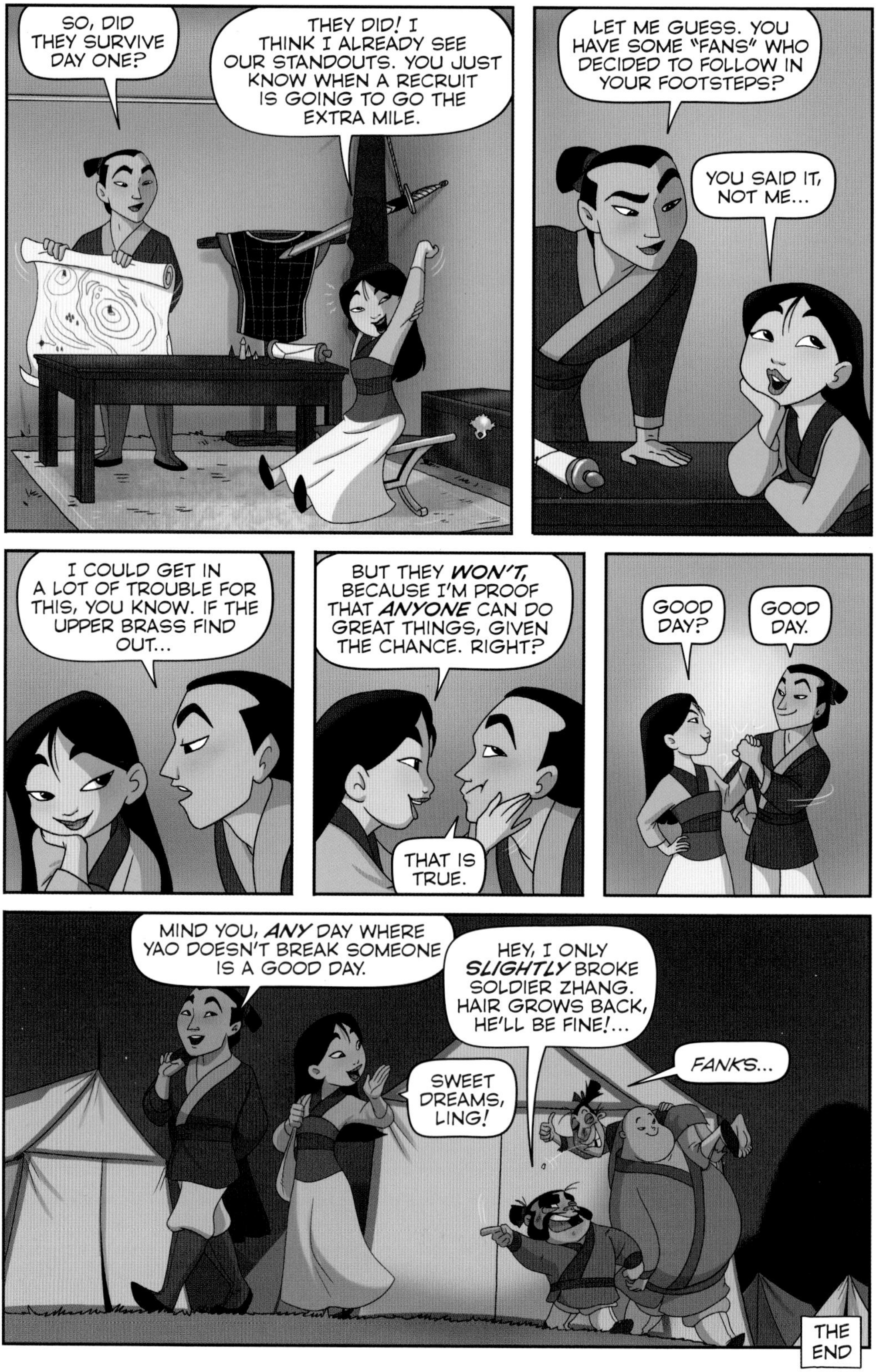
SO, DID THEY SURVIVE DAY ONE?
THEY DID! I THINK I ALREADY SEE OUR STANDOUTS. YOU JUST KNOW WHEN A RECRUIT IS GOING TO GO THE EXTRA MILE.
LET ME GUESS. YOU HAVE SOME "FANS" WHO DECIDED TO FOLLOW IN YOUR FOOTSTEPS?
YOU SAID IT, NOT ME...
I COULD GET IN A LOT OF TROUBLE FOR THIS, YOU KNOW. IF THE UPPER BRASS FIND OUT...
BUT THEY *WON'T*, BECAUSE I'M PROOF THAT *ANYONE* CAN DO GREAT THINGS, GIVEN THE CHANCE. RIGHT?
THAT IS TRUE.
GOOD DAY?
GOOD DAY.
MIND YOU, *ANY* DAY WHERE YAO DOESN'T BREAK SOMEONE IS A GOOD DAY.
HEY, I ONLY *SLIGHTLY* BROKE SOLDIER ZHANG. HAIR GROWS BACK, HE'LL BE FINE!...
SWEET DREAMS, LING!
FANKS...
THE END

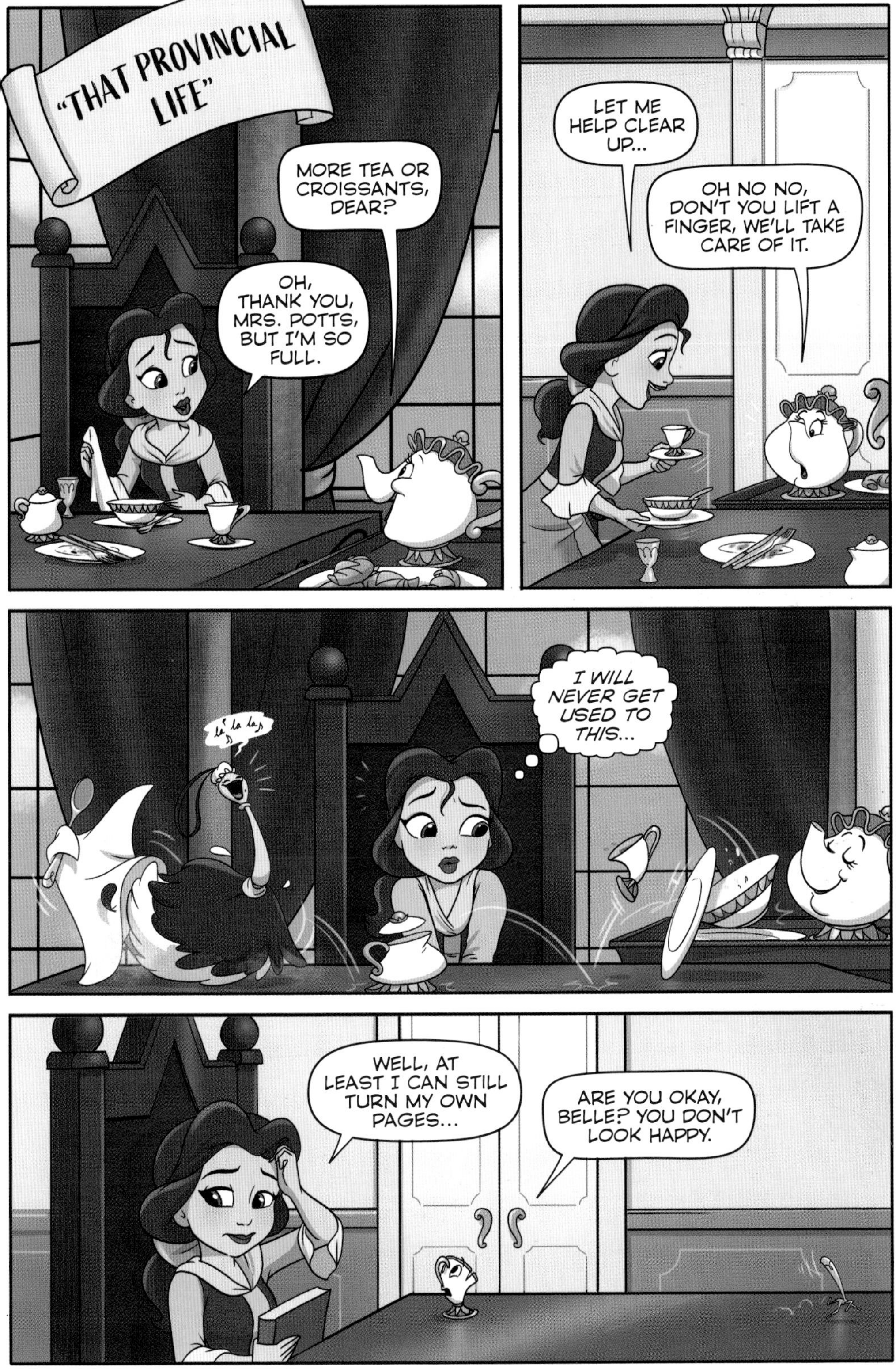
"THAT PROVINCIAL LIFE"
MORE TEA OR CROISSANTS, DEAR?
OH, THANK YOU, MRS. POTTS, BUT I'M SO FULL.
LET ME HELP CLEAR UP...
OH NO NO, DON'T YOU LIFT A FINGER, WE'LL TAKE CARE OF IT.
I WILL NEVER GET USED TO THIS...
WELL, AT LEAST I CAN STILL TURN MY OWN PAGES...
ARE YOU OKAY, BELLE? YOU DON'T LOOK HAPPY.

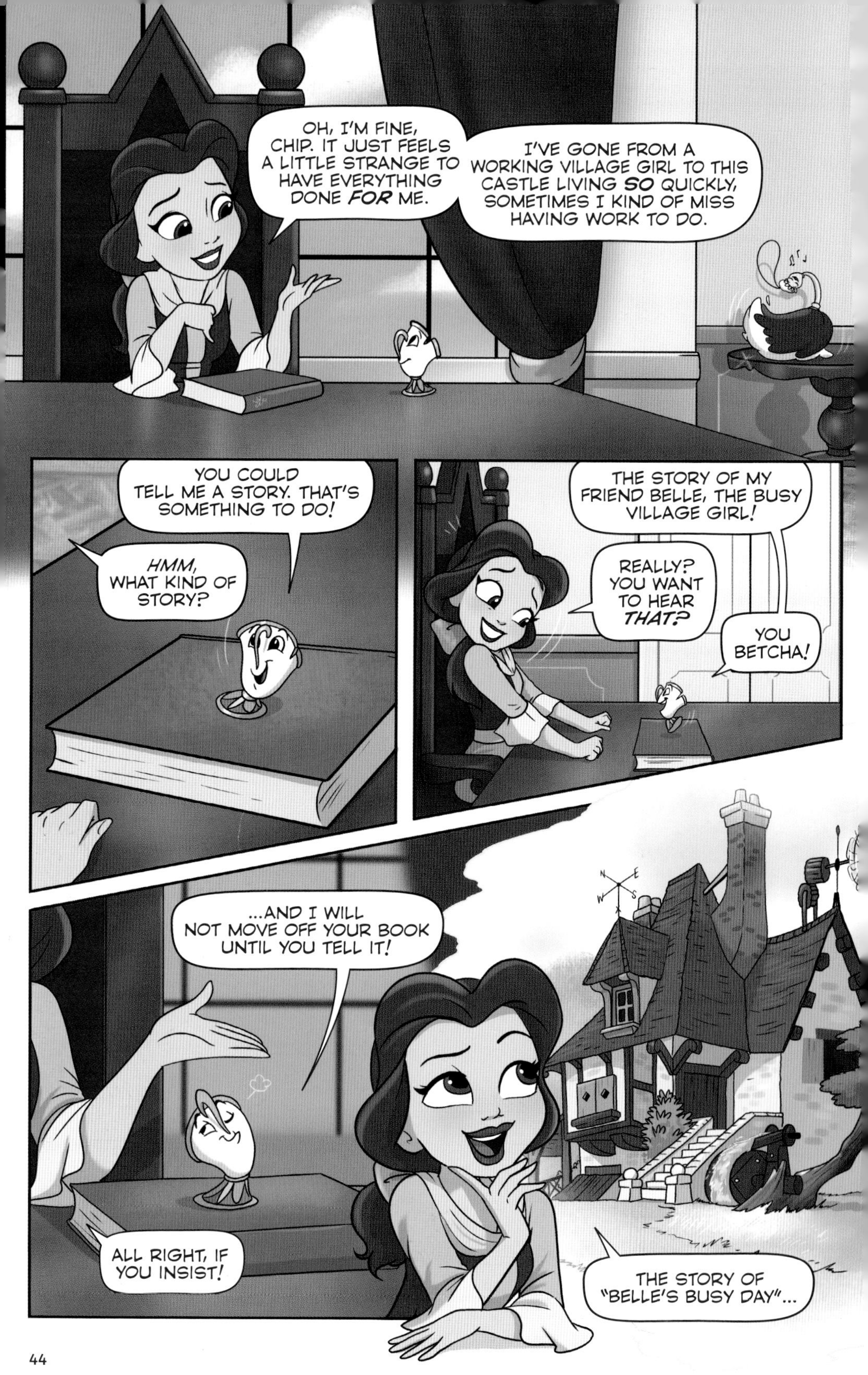
OH, I'M FINE, CHIP. IT JUST FEELS A LITTLE STRANGE TO HAVE EVERYTHING DONE FOR ME.
I'VE GONE FROM A WORKING VILLAGE GIRL TO THIS CASTLE LIVING SO QUICKLY, SOMETIMES I KIND OF MISS HAVING WORK TO DO.
YOU COULD TELL ME A STORY. THAT'S SOMETHING TO DO!
HMM, WHAT KIND OF STORY?
THE STORY OF MY FRIEND BELLE, THE BUSY VILLAGE GIRL!
REALLY? YOU WANT TO HEAR THAT?
YOU BETCHA!
...AND I WILL NOT MOVE OFF YOUR BOOK UNTIL YOU TELL IT!
ALL RIGHT, IF YOU INSIST!
THE STORY OF "BELLE'S BUSY DAY"...

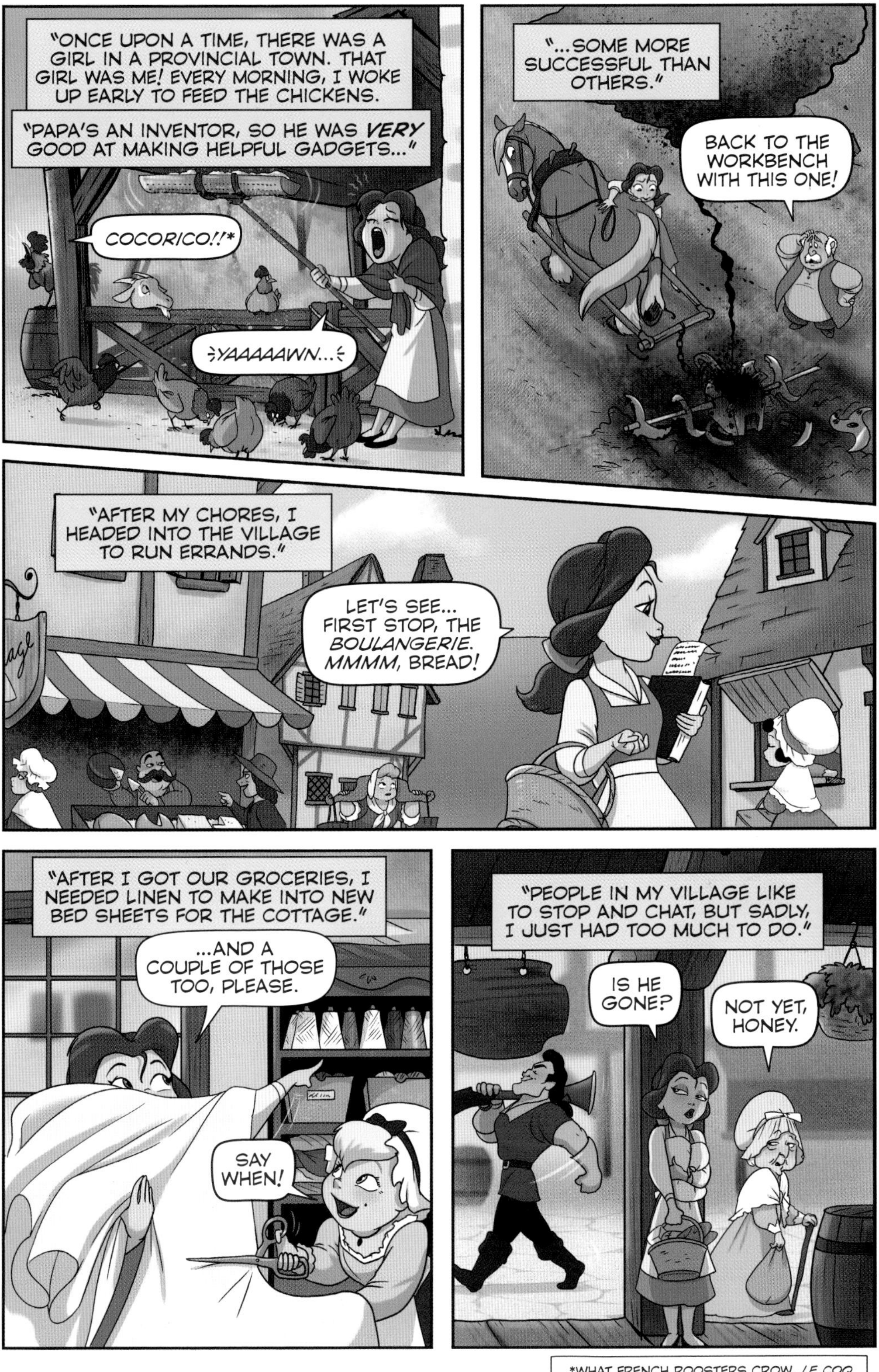
"ONCE UPON A TIME, THERE WAS A GIRL IN A PROVINCIAL TOWN. THAT GIRL WAS ME! EVERY MORNING, I WOKE UP EARLY TO FEED THE CHICKENS.
"PAPA'S AN INVENTOR, SO HE WAS *VERY* GOOD AT MAKING HELPFUL GADGETS..."
*COCORICO!!**
YAAAAAWN...
"...SOME MORE SUCCESSFUL THAN OTHERS."
BACK TO THE WORKBENCH WITH THIS ONE!
"AFTER MY CHORES, I HEADED INTO THE VILLAGE TO RUN ERRANDS."
LET'S SEE... FIRST STOP, THE *BOULANGERIE.* *MMMM*, BREAD!
"AFTER I GOT OUR GROCERIES, I NEEDED LINEN TO MAKE INTO NEW BED SHEETS FOR THE COTTAGE."
...AND A COUPLE OF THOSE TOO, PLEASE.
SAY WHEN!
"PEOPLE IN MY VILLAGE LIKE TO STOP AND CHAT, BUT SADLY, I JUST HAD TOO MUCH TO DO."
IS HE GONE?
NOT YET, HONEY.

*WHAT FRENCH ROOSTERS CROW. *LE COQ GAULOIS* IS A NATIONAL SYMBOL OF FRANCE.

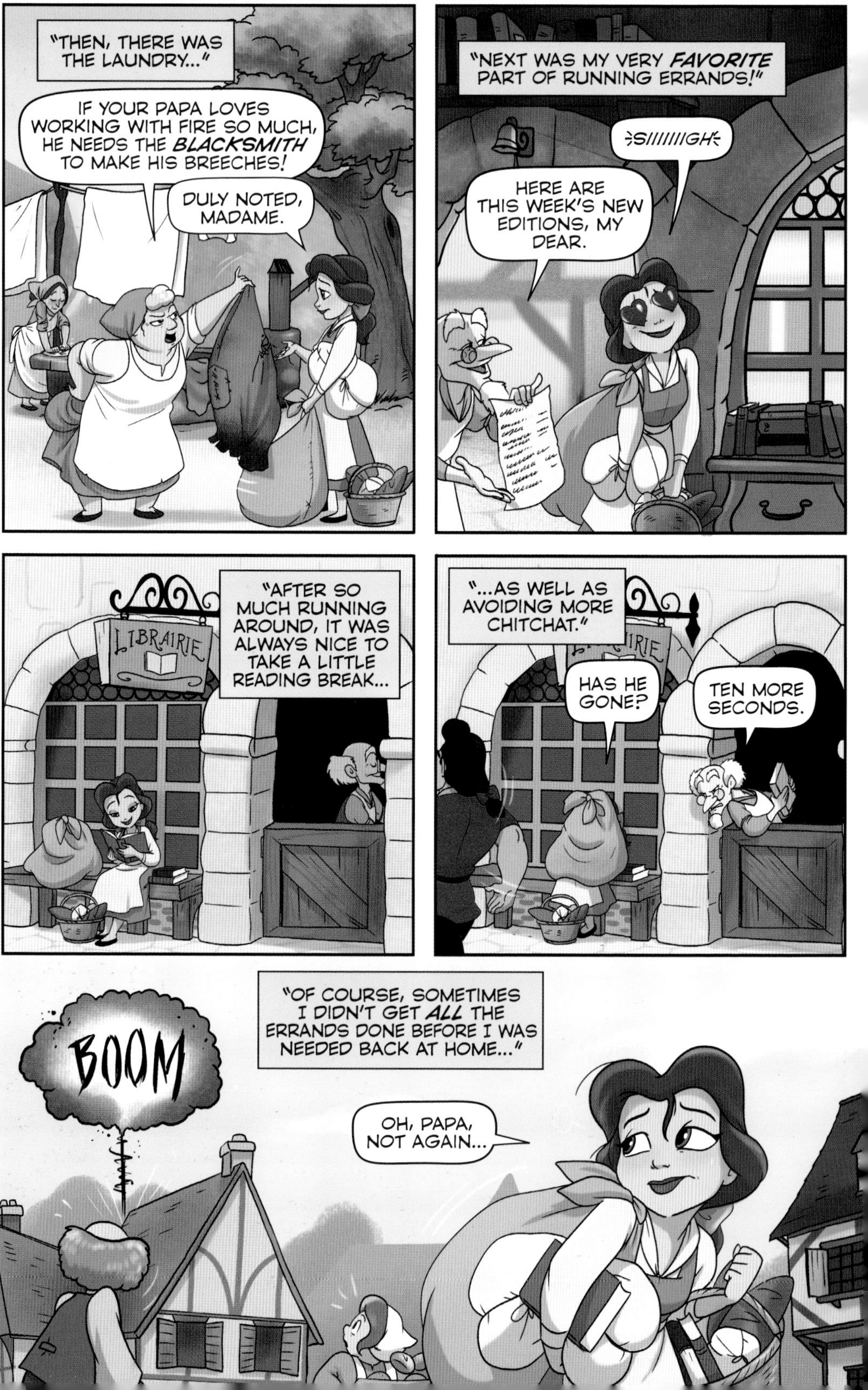
"THEN, THERE WAS THE LAUNDRY..."
IF YOUR PAPA LOVES WORKING WITH FIRE SO MUCH, HE NEEDS THE *BLACKSMITH* TO MAKE HIS BREECHES!
DULY NOTED, MADAME.
"NEXT WAS MY VERY *FAVORITE* PART OF RUNNING ERRANDS!"
HERE ARE THIS WEEK'S NEW EDITIONS, MY DEAR.
SIIIIIIIGH
"AFTER SO MUCH RUNNING AROUND, IT WAS ALWAYS NICE TO TAKE A LITTLE READING BREAK...
LIBRAIRIE
"...AS WELL AS AVOIDING MORE CHITCHAT."
HAS HE GONE?
TEN MORE SECONDS.
"OF COURSE, SOMETIMES I DIDN'T GET *ALL* THE ERRANDS DONE BEFORE I WAS NEEDED BACK AT HOME..."
BOOM
OH, PAPA, NOT AGAIN...

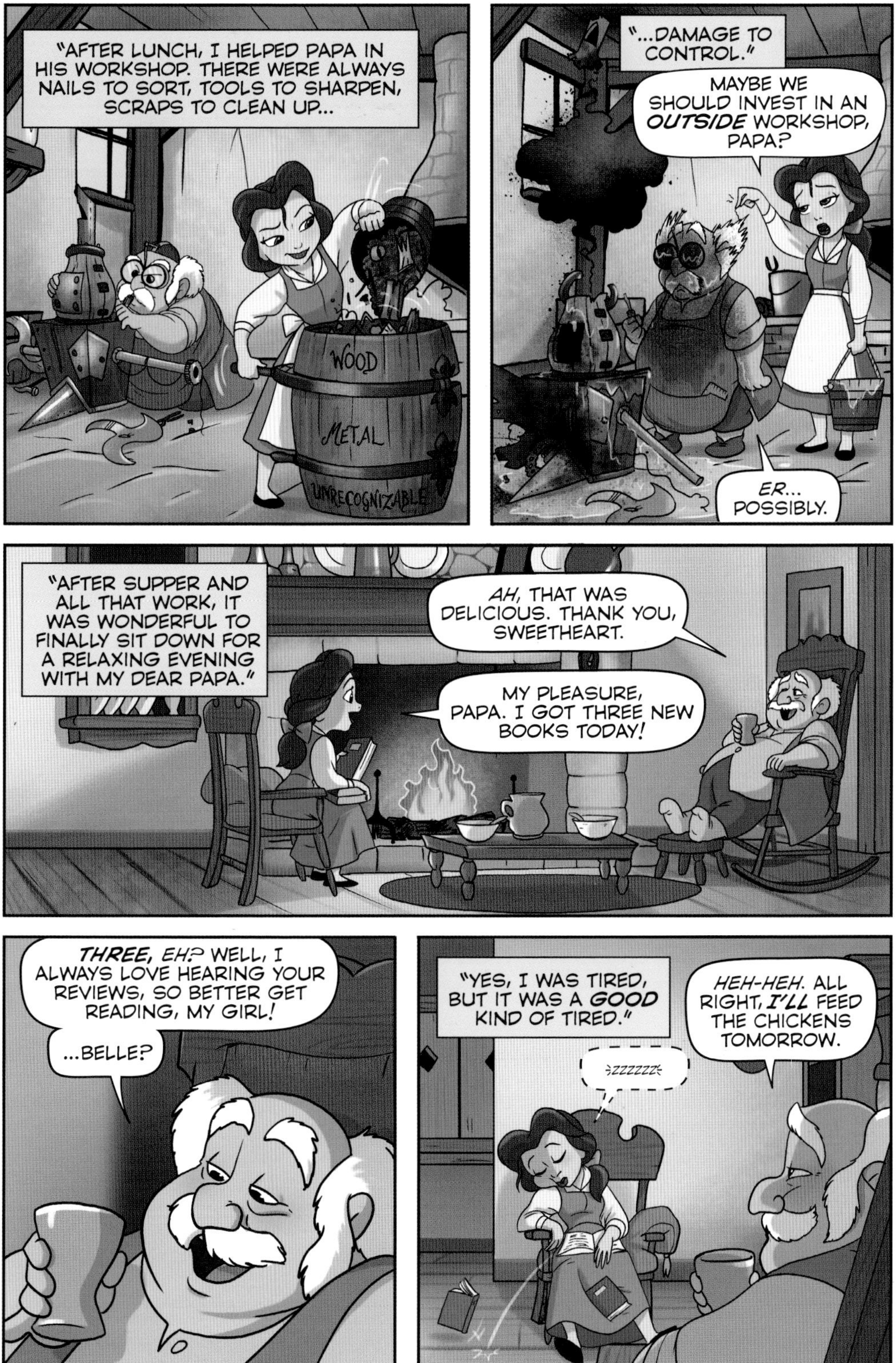
"AFTER LUNCH, I HELPED PAPA IN HIS WORKSHOP. THERE WERE ALWAYS NAILS TO SORT, TOOLS TO SHARPEN, SCRAPS TO CLEAN UP...
WOOD
METAL
UNRECOGNIZABLE
"...DAMAGE TO CONTROL."
MAYBE WE SHOULD INVEST IN AN *OUTSIDE* WORKSHOP, PAPA?
ER... POSSIBLY.
"AFTER SUPPER AND ALL THAT WORK, IT WAS WONDERFUL TO FINALLY SIT DOWN FOR A RELAXING EVENING WITH MY DEAR PAPA."
AH, THAT WAS DELICIOUS. THANK YOU, SWEETHEART.
MY PLEASURE, PAPA. I GOT THREE NEW BOOKS TODAY!
THREE, *EH?* WELL, I ALWAYS LOVE HEARING YOUR REVIEWS, SO BETTER GET READING, MY GIRL!
...BELLE?
"YES, I WAS TIRED, BUT IT WAS A ***GOOD*** KIND OF TIRED."
ZZZZZZ
HEH-HEH. ALL RIGHT, ***I'LL*** FEED THE CHICKENS TOMORROW.

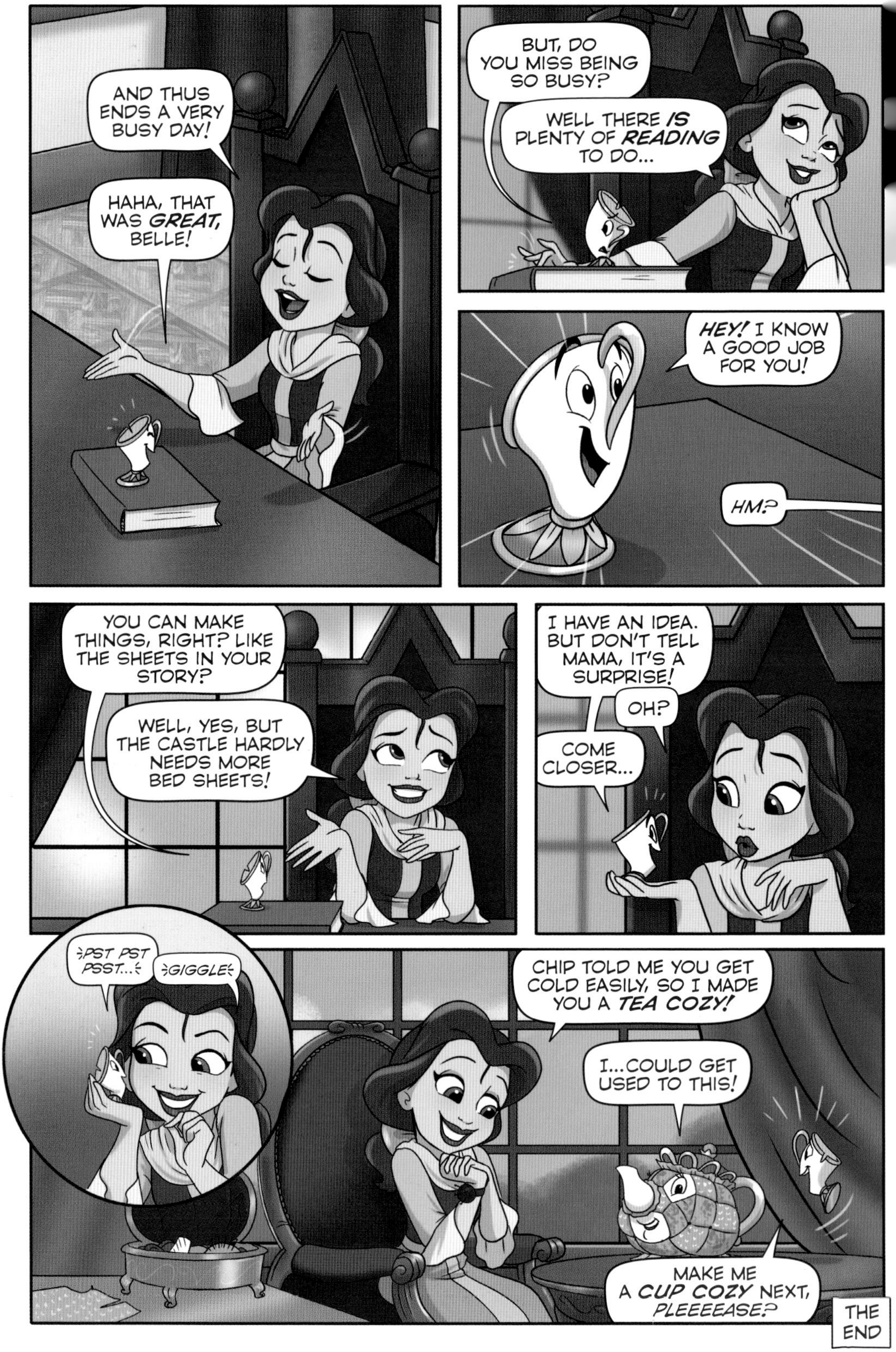
AND THUS ENDS A VERY BUSY DAY!
HAHA, THAT WAS GREAT, BELLE!
BUT, DO YOU MISS BEING SO BUSY?
WELL THERE IS PLENTY OF READING TO DO...
HEY! I KNOW A GOOD JOB FOR YOU!
HM?
YOU CAN MAKE THINGS, RIGHT? LIKE THE SHEETS IN YOUR STORY?
WELL, YES, BUT THE CASTLE HARDLY NEEDS MORE BED SHEETS!
I HAVE AN IDEA. BUT DON'T TELL MAMA, IT'S A SURPRISE!
OH?
COME CLOSER...
PST PST PSST...
GIGGLE
CHIP TOLD ME YOU GET COLD EASILY, SO I MADE YOU A TEA COZY!
I...COULD GET USED TO THIS!
MAKE ME A CUP COZY NEXT, PLEEEEASE?
THE END

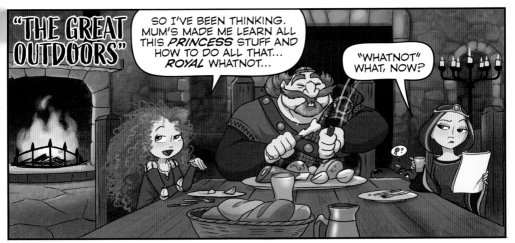

"THE GREAT OUTDOORS"

SO I'VE BEEN THINKING. MUM'S MADE ME LEARN ALL THIS *PRINCESS* STUFF AND HOW TO DO ALL THAT... *ROYAL* WHATNOT...

"WHATNOT" WHAT, NOW?

BUT WHAT I *COULD* USE, THOUGH, ARE SOME MORE LESSONS IN... *OUTDOORSY* THINGS!

COME ON, DA, YOU DO LOTS OF SPORTS! FALCONRY! OR RANGING! YOU'RE PRETTY GOOD AT THE OL' SHINTY FOR SOMEONE WITH ONLY ONE LEG!

YER ALREADY THE FINEST ARCHER IN THE KINGDOM, LASSIE! WHAT D'YE NEED *ME* FER?

AYE, IT HELPS WHEN I CAN USE *THIS* TO HIT THE BALL!

‡SNORK‡ SO MUCH FOR THE RULES!

CAN WE HAVE *ONE* DINNER WITHOUT FEET ON THE TABLE?

CHOMP!

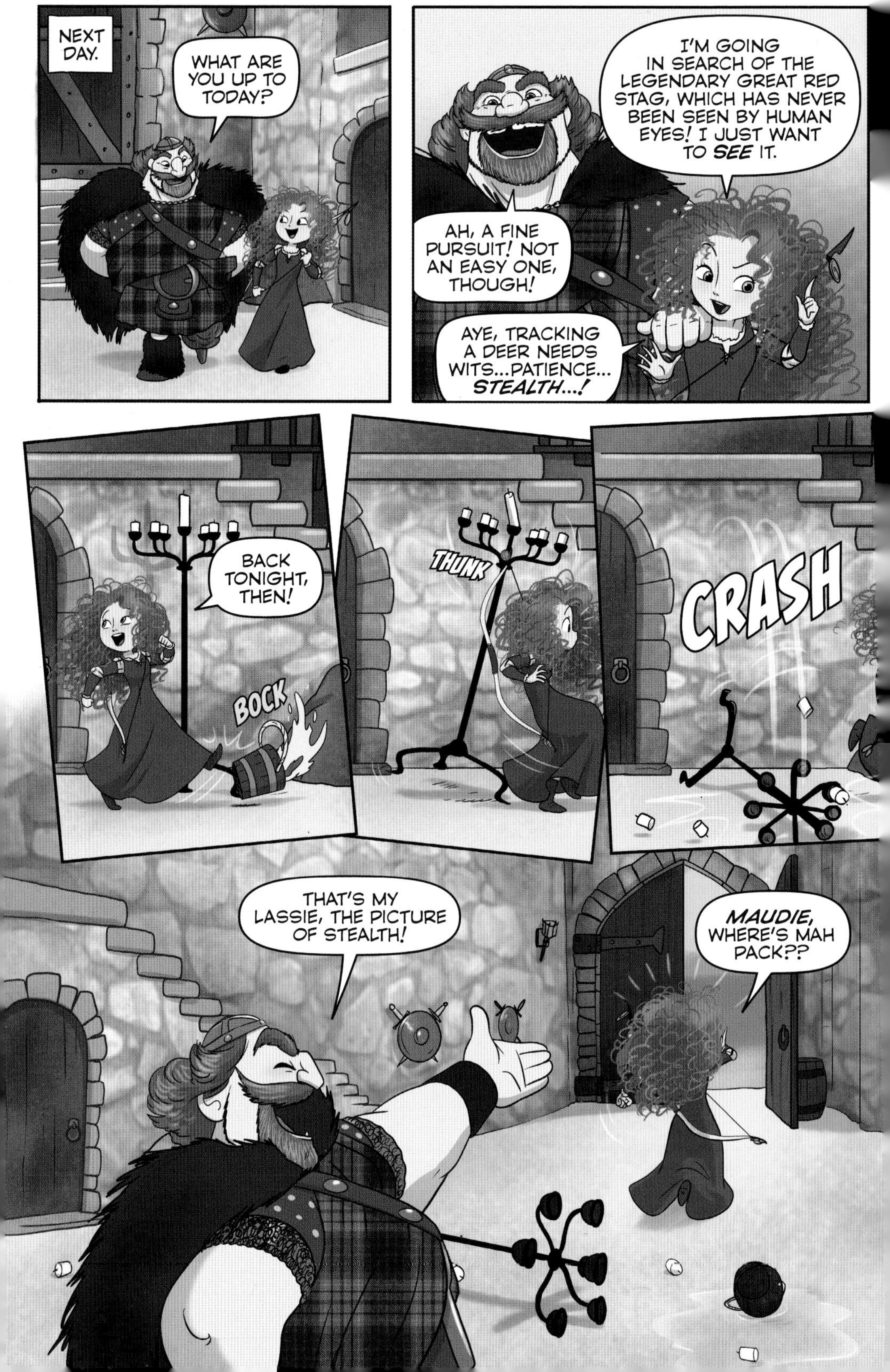
NEXT DAY.
WHAT ARE YOU UP TO TODAY?
I'M GOING IN SEARCH OF THE LEGENDARY GREAT RED STAG, WHICH HAS NEVER BEEN SEEN BY HUMAN EYES! I JUST WANT TO SEE IT.
AH, A FINE PURSUIT! NOT AN EASY ONE, THOUGH!
AYE, TRACKING A DEER NEEDS WITS...PATIENCE... STEALTH...!
BACK TONIGHT, THEN!
BOCK
THUNK
CRASH
THAT'S MY LASSIE, THE PICTURE OF STEALTH!
MAUDIE, WHERE'S MAH PACK??

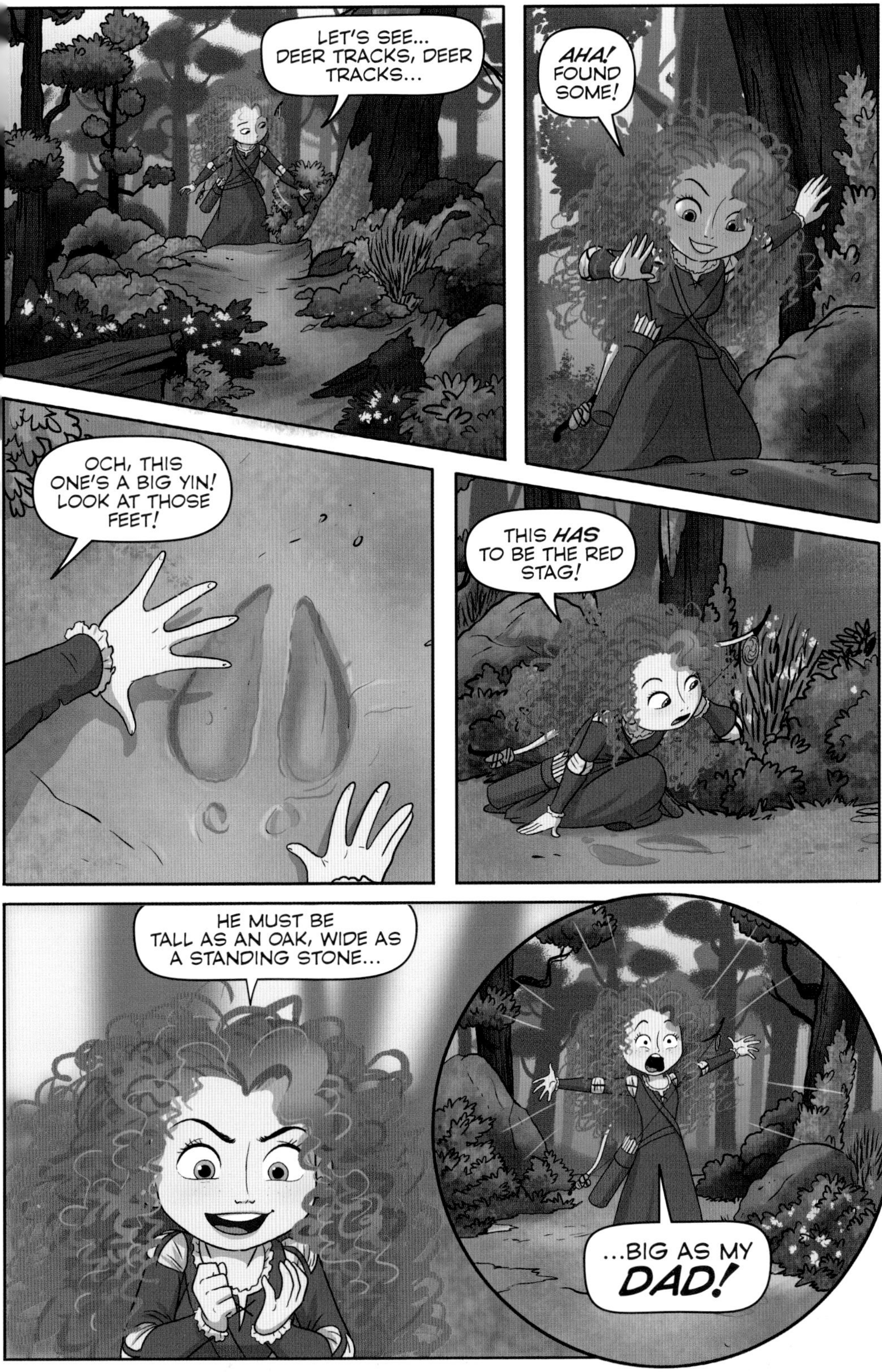
LET'S SEE... DEER TRACKS, DEER TRACKS...
AHA! FOUND SOME!
OCH, THIS ONE'S A BIG YIN! LOOK AT THOSE FEET!
THIS HAS TO BE THE RED STAG!
HE MUST BE TALL AS AN OAK, WIDE AS A STANDING STONE...
...BIG AS MY DAD!

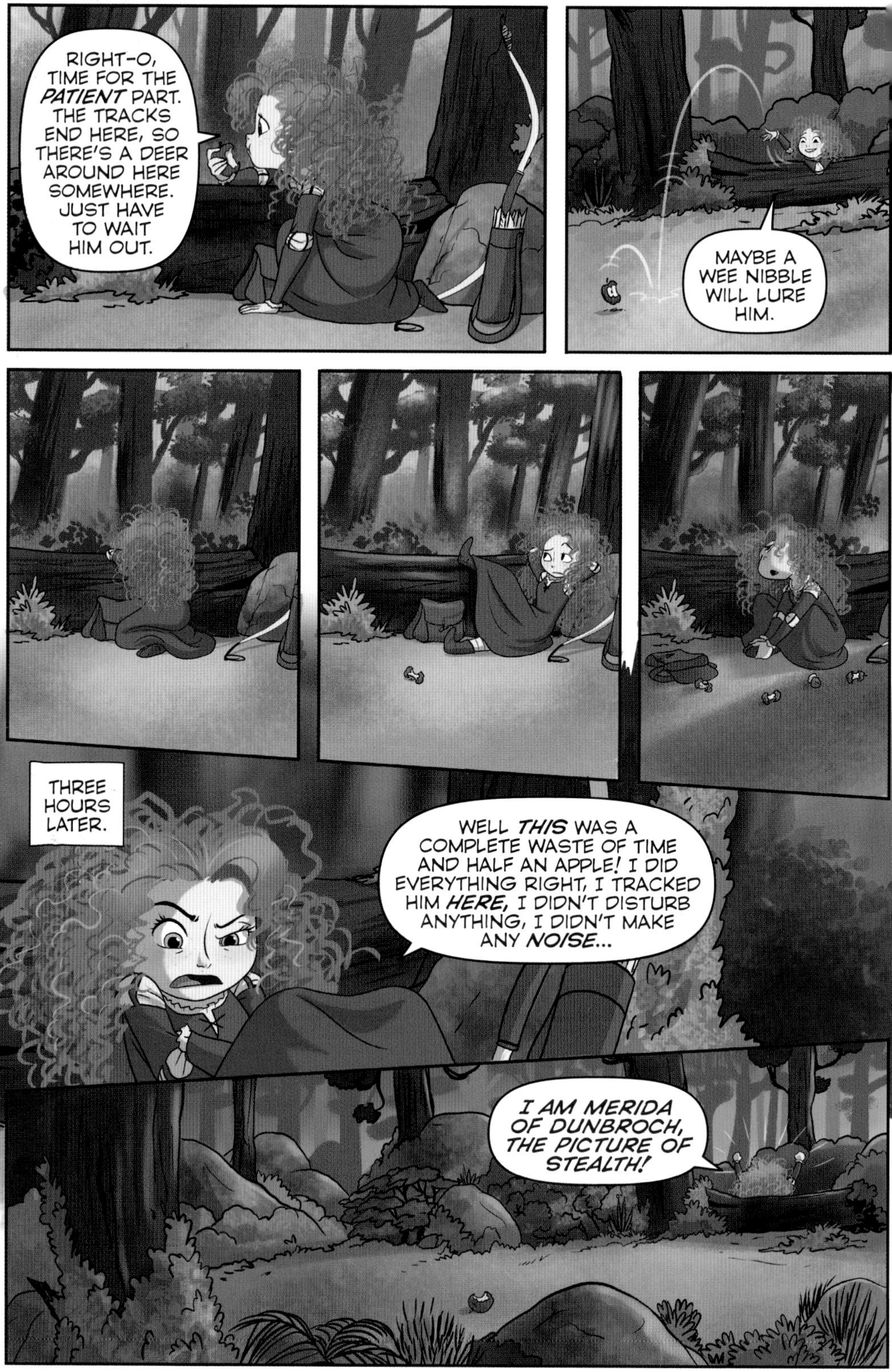

RIGHT-O, TIME FOR THE *PATIENT* PART. THE TRACKS END HERE, SO THERE'S A DEER AROUND HERE SOMEWHERE. JUST HAVE TO WAIT HIM OUT.
MAYBE A WEE NIBBLE WILL LURE HIM.
THREE HOURS LATER.
WELL *THIS* WAS A COMPLETE WASTE OF TIME AND HALF AN APPLE! I DID EVERYTHING RIGHT, I TRACKED HIM *HERE*, I DIDN'T DISTURB ANYTHING, I DIDN'T MAKE ANY *NOISE*...
I AM MERIDA OF DUNBROCH, THE PICTURE OF STEALTH!

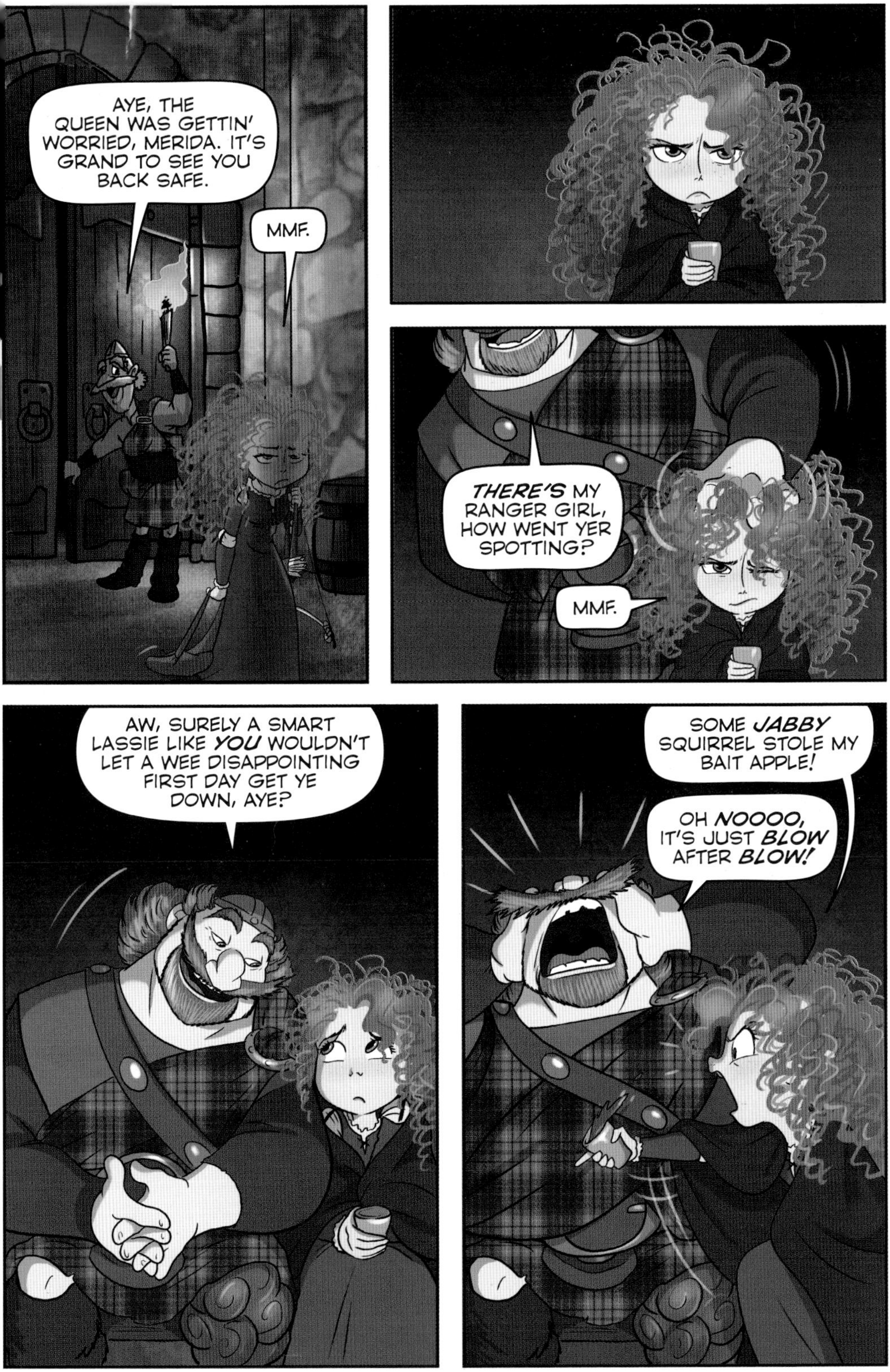
AYE, THE QUEEN WAS GETTIN' WORRIED, MERIDA. IT'S GRAND TO SEE YOU BACK SAFE.
MMF.
THERE'S MY RANGER GIRL, HOW WENT YER SPOTTING?
MMF.
AW, SURELY A SMART LASSIE LIKE YOU WOULDN'T LET A WEE DISAPPOINTING FIRST DAY GET YE DOWN, AYE?
SOME JABBY SQUIRREL STOLE MY BAIT APPLE!
OH NOOOO, IT'S JUST BLOW AFTER BLOW!

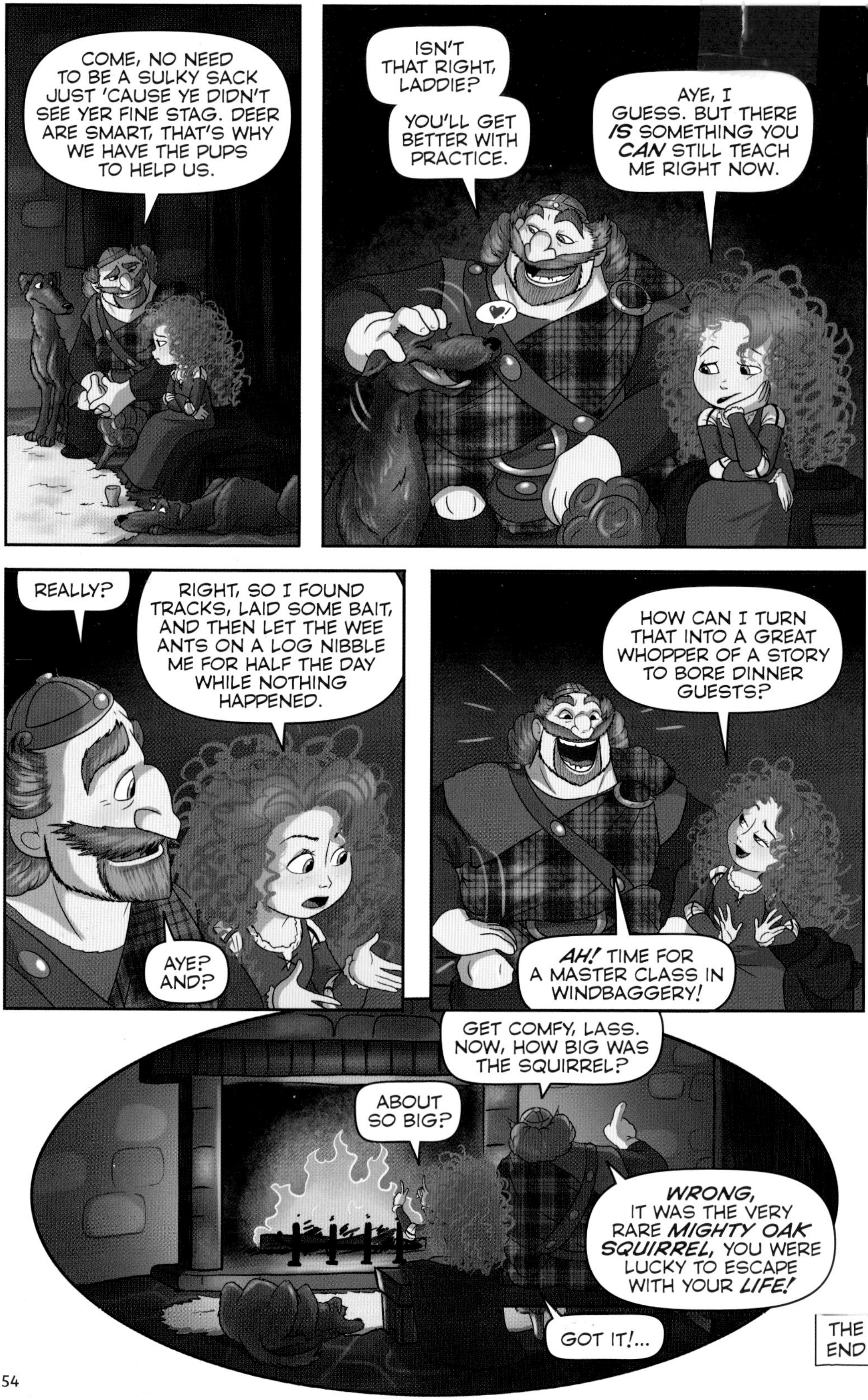
COME, NO NEED TO BE A SULKY SACK JUST 'CAUSE YE DIDN'T SEE YER FINE STAG. DEER ARE SMART, THAT'S WHY WE HAVE THE PUPS TO HELP US.
ISN'T THAT RIGHT, LADDIE?
YOU'LL GET BETTER WITH PRACTICE.
AYE, I GUESS. BUT THERE *IS* SOMETHING YOU *CAN* STILL TEACH ME RIGHT NOW.
REALLY?
RIGHT, SO I FOUND TRACKS, LAID SOME BAIT, AND THEN LET THE WEE ANTS ON A LOG NIBBLE ME FOR HALF THE DAY WHILE NOTHING HAPPENED.
AYE? AND?
HOW CAN I TURN THAT INTO A GREAT WHOPPER OF A STORY TO BORE DINNER GUESTS?
AH! TIME FOR A MASTER CLASS IN WINDBAGGERY!
GET COMFY, LASS. NOW, HOW BIG WAS THE SQUIRREL?
ABOUT SO BIG?
WRONG, IT WAS THE VERY RARE *MIGHTY OAK SQUIRREL,* YOU WERE LUCKY TO ESCAPE WITH YOUR *LIFE!*
GOT IT!...
THE END

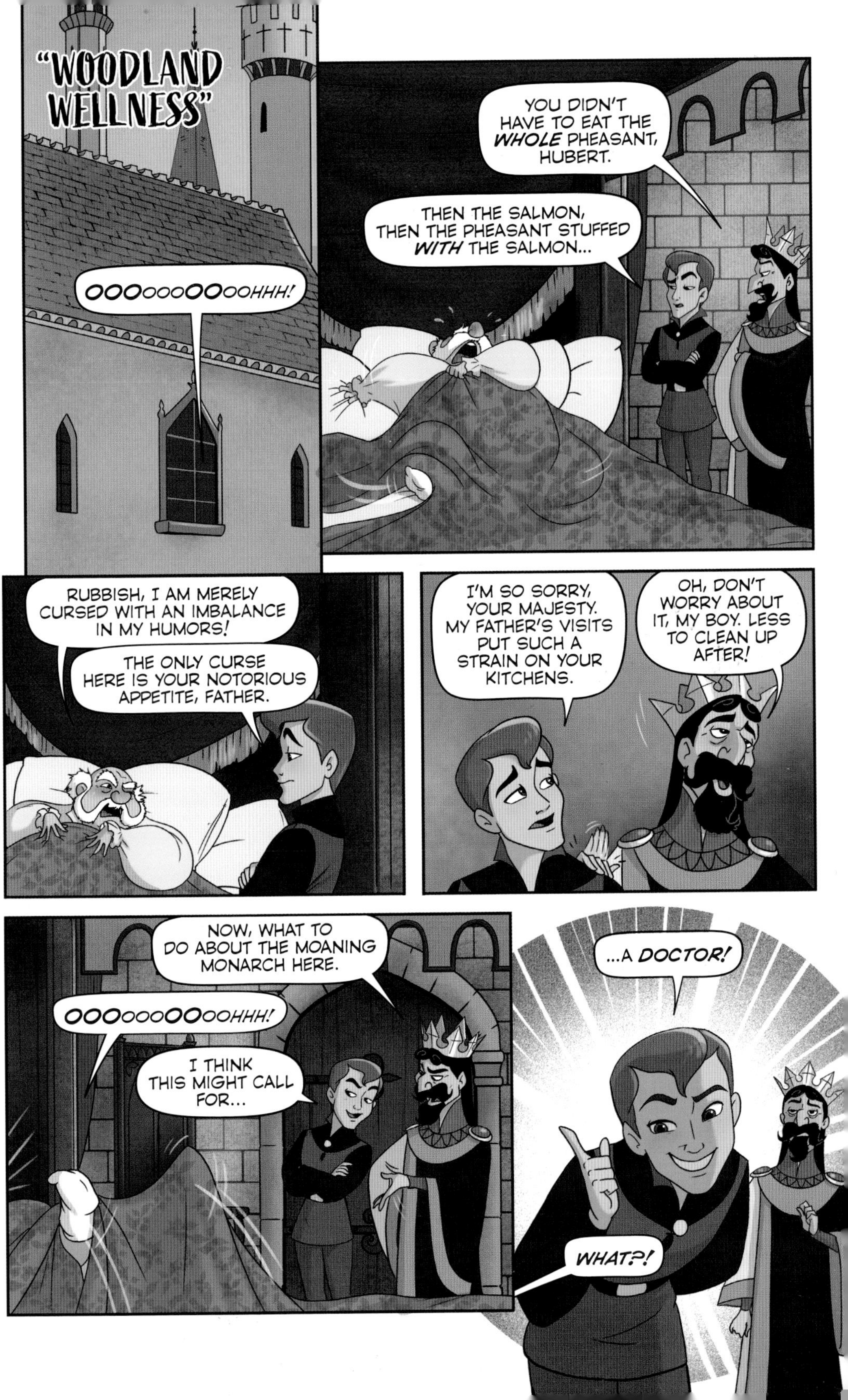
"WOODLAND WELLNESS"
OOOoooOOoohhh!
YOU DIDN'T HAVE TO EAT THE *WHOLE* PHEASANT, HUBERT.
THEN THE SALMON, THEN THE PHEASANT STUFFED *WITH* THE SALMON...
RUBBISH, I AM MERELY CURSED WITH AN IMBALANCE IN MY HUMORS!
THE ONLY CURSE HERE IS YOUR NOTORIOUS APPETITE, FATHER.
I'M SO SORRY, YOUR MAJESTY. MY FATHER'S VISITS PUT SUCH A STRAIN ON YOUR KITCHENS.
OH, DON'T WORRY ABOUT IT, MY BOY. LESS TO CLEAN UP AFTER!
NOW, WHAT TO DO ABOUT THE MOANING MONARCH HERE.
OOOoooOOoohhh!
I THINK THIS MIGHT CALL FOR...
...A *DOCTOR!*
WHAT?!

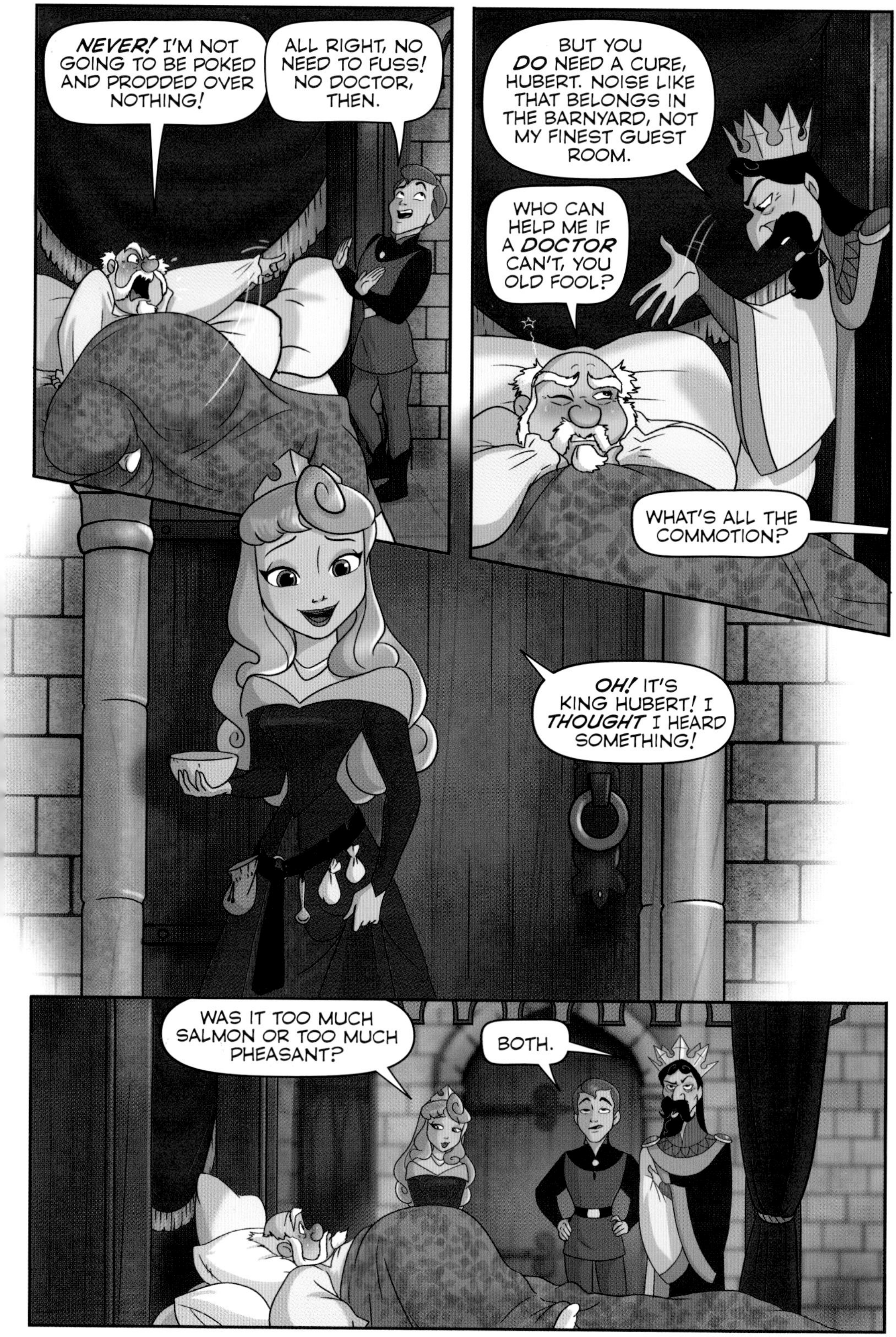
NEVER! I'M NOT GOING TO BE POKED AND PRODDED OVER NOTHING!
ALL RIGHT, NO NEED TO FUSS! NO DOCTOR, THEN.
BUT YOU DO NEED A CURE, HUBERT. NOISE LIKE THAT BELONGS IN THE BARNYARD, NOT MY FINEST GUEST ROOM.
WHO CAN HELP ME IF A DOCTOR CAN'T, YOU OLD FOOL?
WHAT'S ALL THE COMMOTION?
OH! IT'S KING HUBERT! I THOUGHT I HEARD SOMETHING!
WAS IT TOO MUCH SALMON OR TOO MUCH PHEASANT?
BOTH.

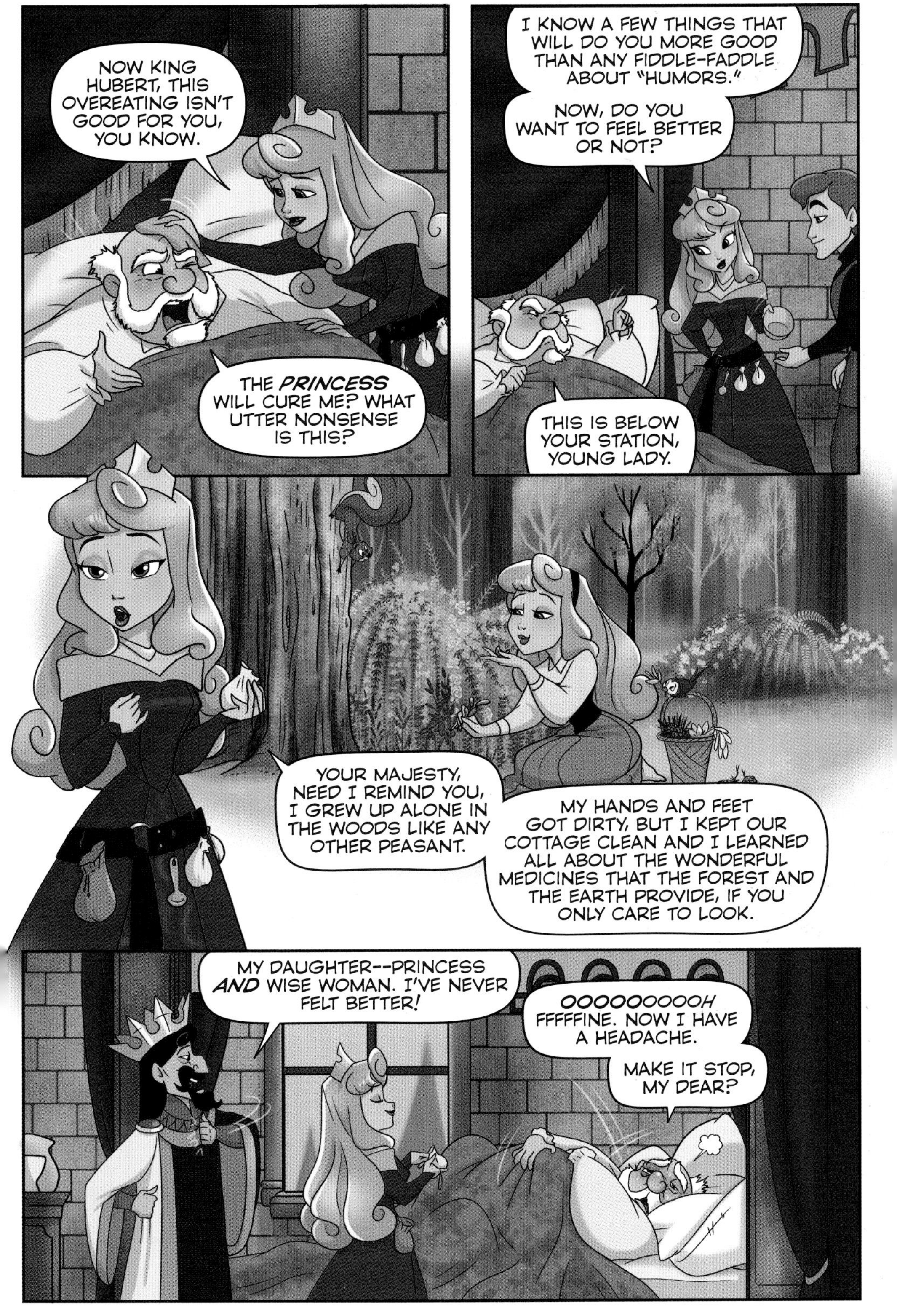
NOW KING HUBERT, THIS OVEREATING ISN'T GOOD FOR YOU, YOU KNOW.
THE *PRINCESS* WILL CURE ME? WHAT UTTER NONSENSE IS THIS?
I KNOW A FEW THINGS THAT WILL DO YOU MORE GOOD THAN ANY FIDDLE-FADDLE ABOUT "HUMORS."
NOW, DO YOU WANT TO FEEL BETTER OR NOT?
THIS IS BELOW YOUR STATION, YOUNG LADY.
YOUR MAJESTY, NEED I REMIND YOU, I GREW UP ALONE IN THE WOODS LIKE ANY OTHER PEASANT.
MY HANDS AND FEET GOT DIRTY, BUT I KEPT OUR COTTAGE CLEAN AND I LEARNED ALL ABOUT THE WONDERFUL MEDICINES THAT THE FOREST AND THE EARTH PROVIDE, IF YOU ONLY CARE TO LOOK.
MY DAUGHTER--PRINCESS *AND* WISE WOMAN. I'VE NEVER FELT BETTER!
OOOOOOOOOH FFFFFINE. NOW I HAVE A HEADACHE.
MAKE IT STOP, MY DEAR?

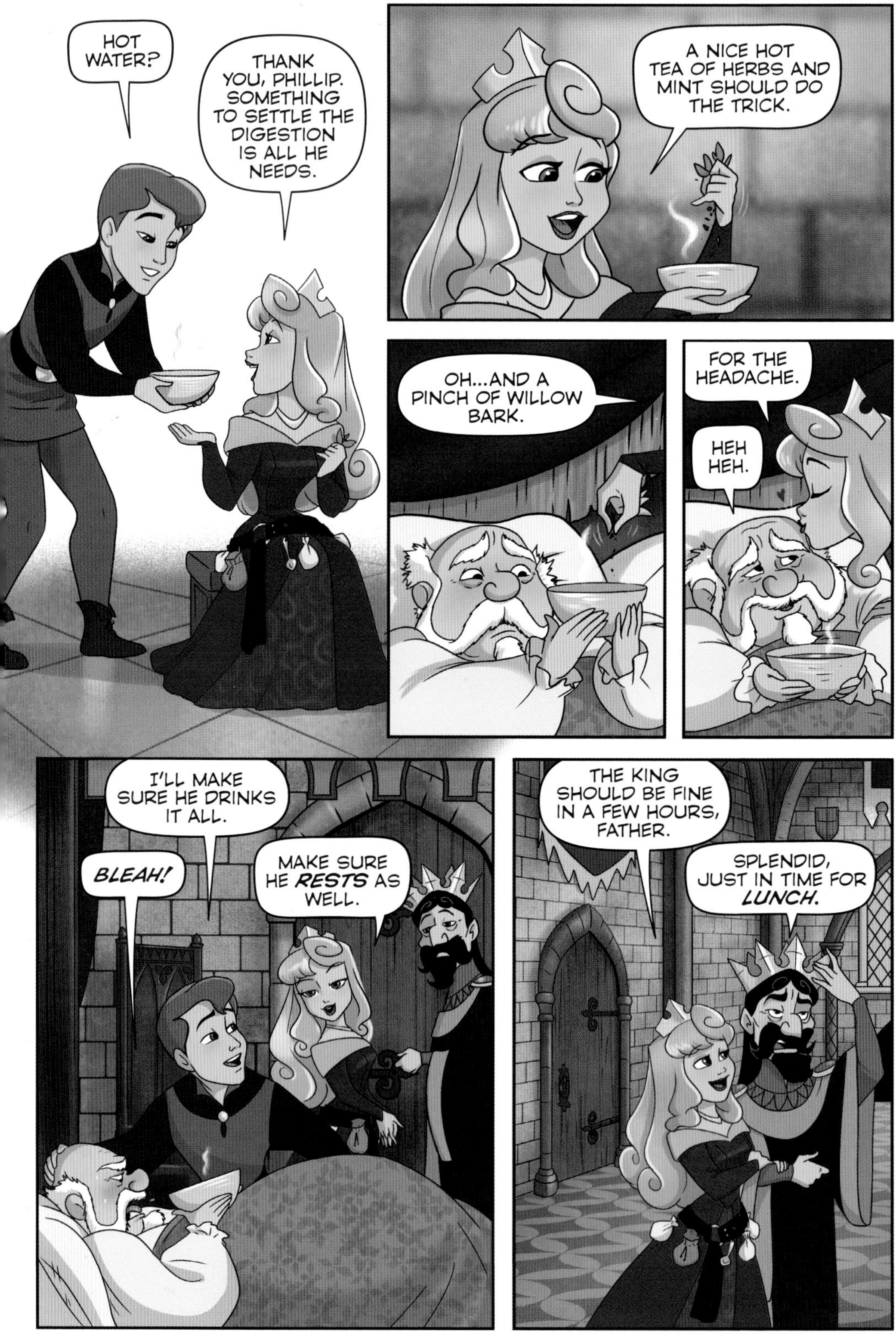
HOT WATER?
THANK YOU, PHILLIP. SOMETHING TO SETTLE THE DIGESTION IS ALL HE NEEDS.
A NICE HOT TEA OF HERBS AND MINT SHOULD DO THE TRICK.
OH...AND A PINCH OF WILLOW BARK.
FOR THE HEADACHE.
HEH HEH.
I'LL MAKE SURE HE DRINKS IT ALL.
BLEAH!
MAKE SURE HE RESTS AS WELL.
THE KING SHOULD BE FINE IN A FEW HOURS, FATHER.
SPLENDID, JUST IN TIME FOR LUNCH.

FEH...TASTED GHASTLY. *AND* I'M SURE THE GOOD LONG NAP I TOOK DIDN'T HURT EITHER.

HOW ARE YOU FEELING, YOUR MAJESTY?

OH, HALE AND HEARTY, MY DEAR! FIT AS A FIDDLE!

A FEW SIMPLE HERBS CAN HELP SO MUCH, YES?

WELL, I'M... GLAD TO HEAR THAT.

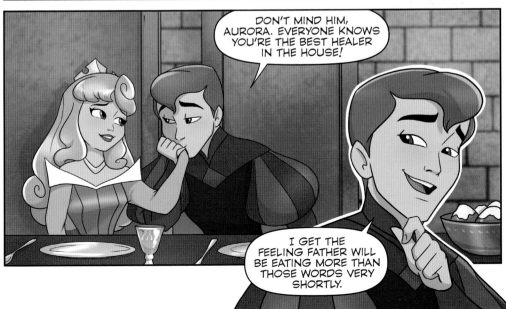

DON'T MIND HIM, AURORA. EVERYONE KNOWS YOU'RE THE BEST HEALER IN THE HOUSE!

I GET THE FEELING FATHER WILL BE EATING MORE THAN THOSE WORDS VERY SHORTLY.

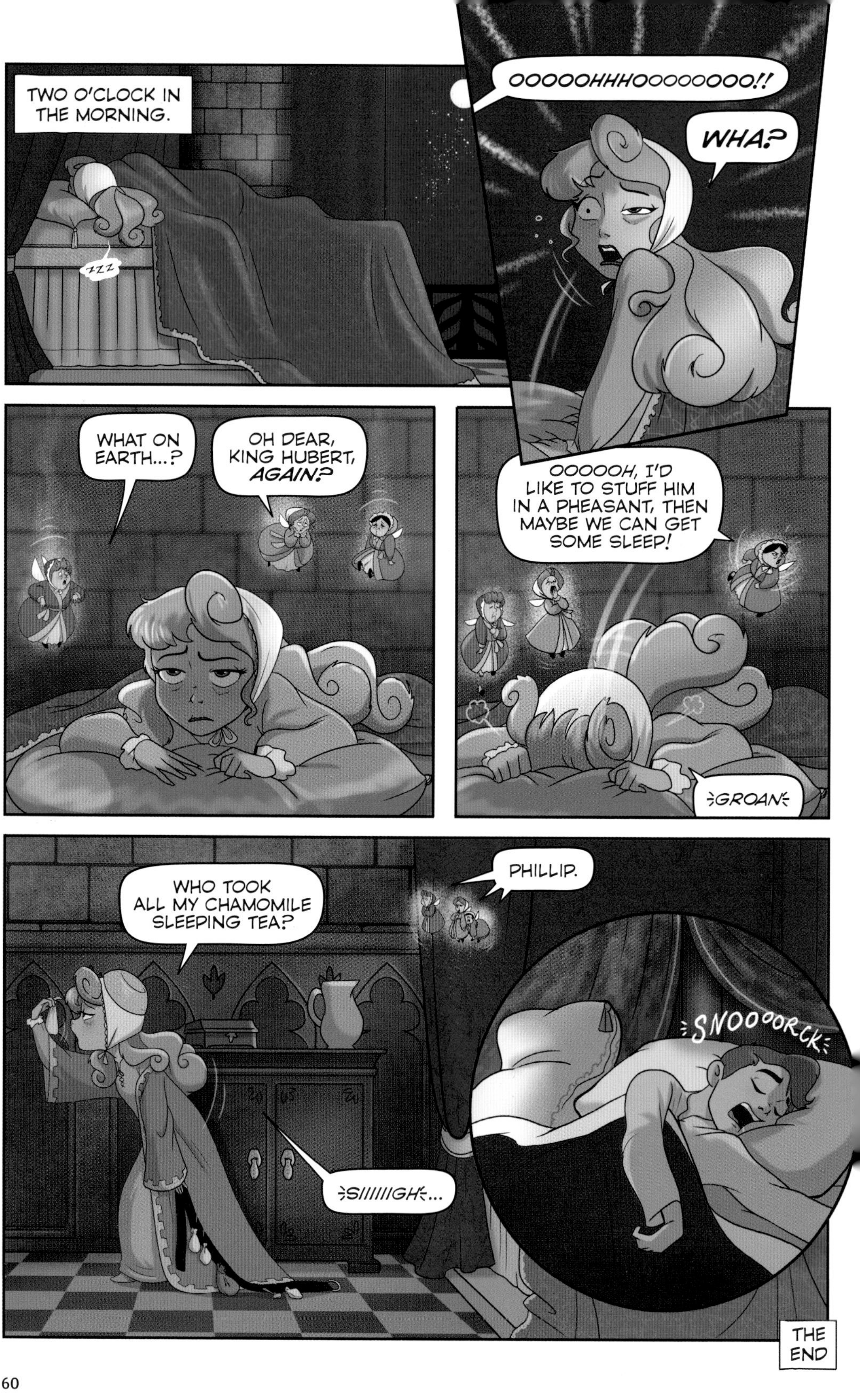
TWO O'CLOCK IN THE MORNING.
ZZZ
OOOOOHHHOOOOOOOO!!
WHA?
WHAT ON EARTH...?
OH DEAR, KING HUBERT, *AGAIN?*
OOOOOH, I'D LIKE TO STUFF HIM IN A PHEASANT, THEN MAYBE WE CAN GET SOME SLEEP!
GROAN
WHO TOOK ALL MY CHAMOMILE SLEEPING TEA?
PHILLIP.
SNOOOORCK
SIIIIIIGH...
THE END

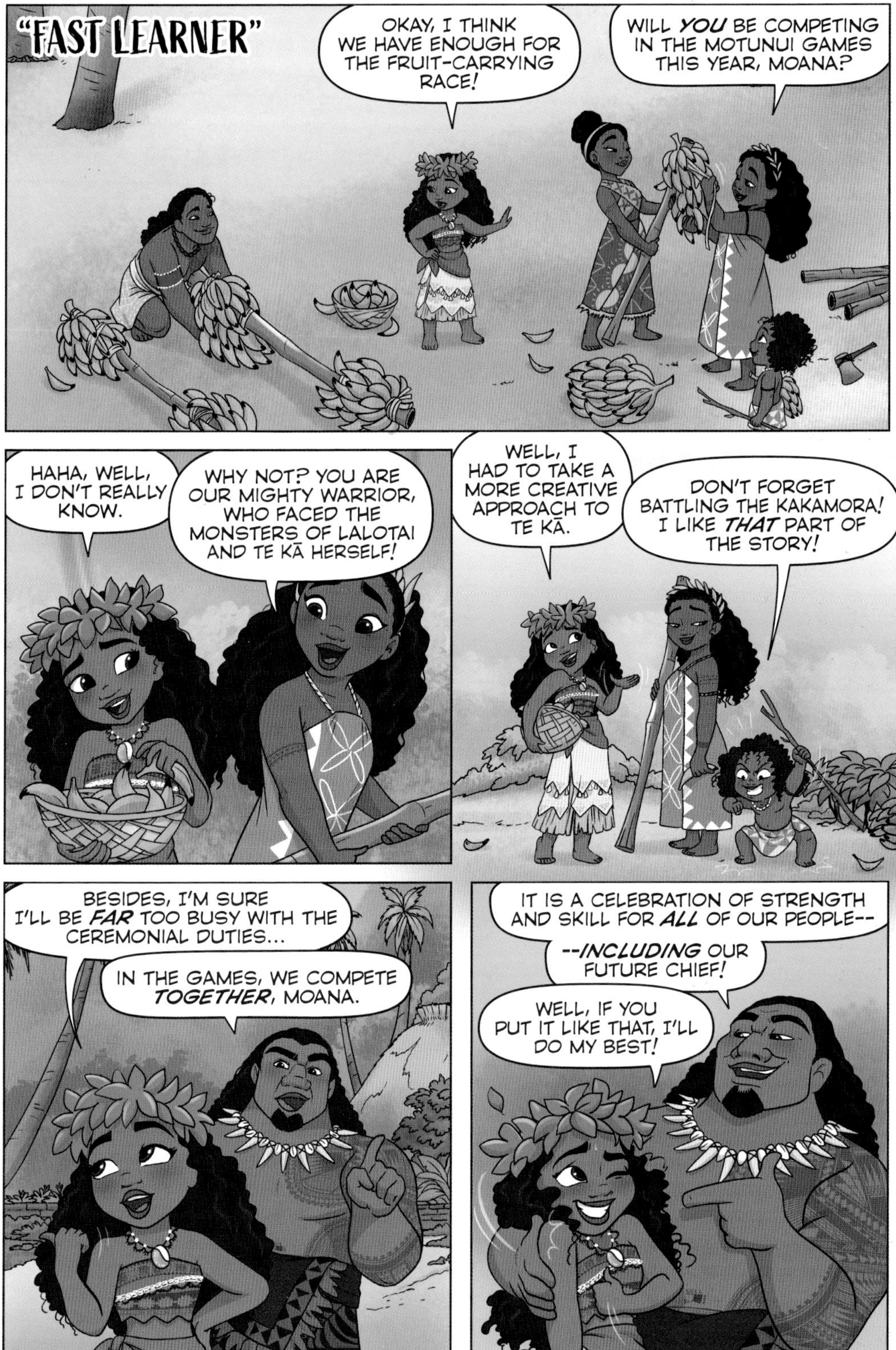
"FAST LEARNER"
OKAY, I THINK WE HAVE ENOUGH FOR THE FRUIT-CARRYING RACE!
WILL YOU BE COMPETING IN THE MOTUNUI GAMES THIS YEAR, MOANA?
HAHA, WELL, I DON'T REALLY KNOW.
WHY NOT? YOU ARE OUR MIGHTY WARRIOR, WHO FACED THE MONSTERS OF LALOTAI AND TE KĀ HERSELF!
WELL, I HAD TO TAKE A MORE CREATIVE APPROACH TO TE KĀ.
DON'T FORGET BATTLING THE KAKAMORA! I LIKE THAT PART OF THE STORY!
BESIDES, I'M SURE I'LL BE FAR TOO BUSY WITH THE CEREMONIAL DUTIES...
IN THE GAMES, WE COMPETE TOGETHER, MOANA.
IT IS A CELEBRATION OF STRENGTH AND SKILL FOR ALL OF OUR PEOPLE--
--INCLUDING OUR FUTURE CHIEF!
WELL, IF YOU PUT IT LIKE THAT, I'LL DO MY BEST!

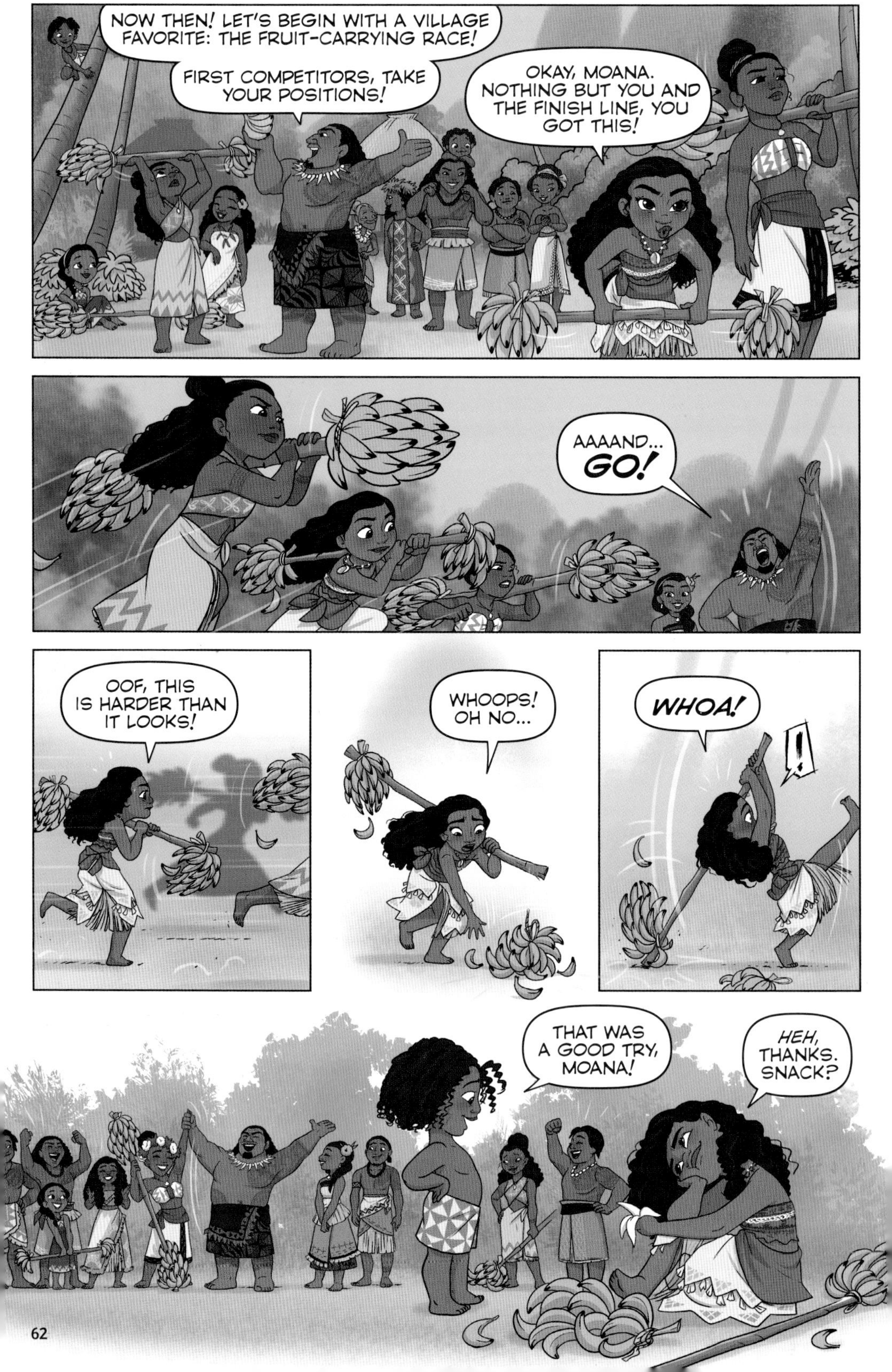
NOW THEN! LET'S BEGIN WITH A VILLAGE FAVORITE: THE FRUIT-CARRYING RACE!
FIRST COMPETITORS, TAKE YOUR POSITIONS!
OKAY, MOANA. NOTHING BUT YOU AND THE FINISH LINE, YOU GOT THIS!
AAAAND... GO!
OOF, THIS IS HARDER THAN IT LOOKS!
WHOOPS! OH NO...
WHOA!
!
THAT WAS A GOOD TRY, MOANA!
HEH, THANKS. SNACK?

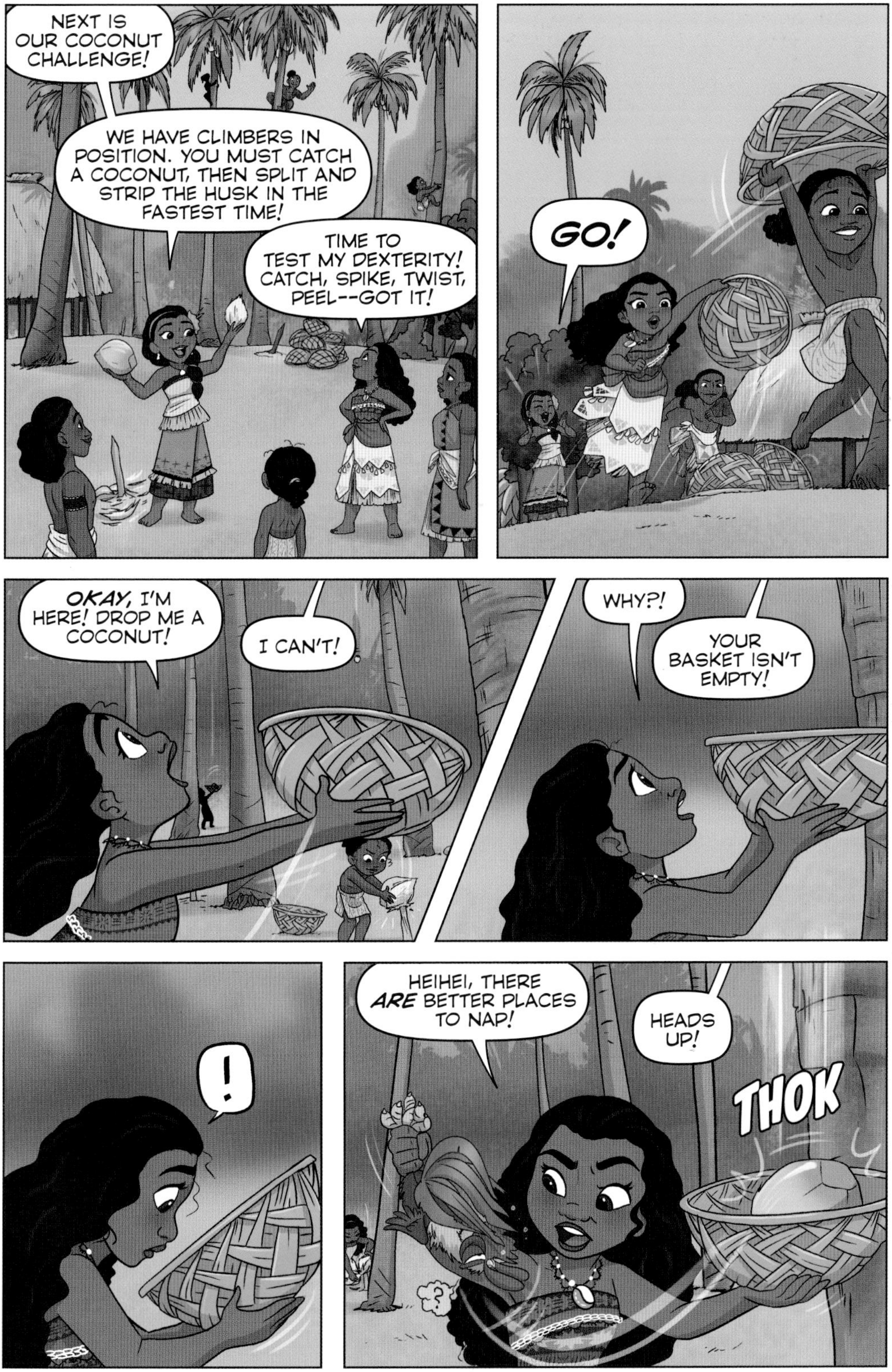
NEXT IS OUR COCONUT CHALLENGE!
WE HAVE CLIMBERS IN POSITION. YOU MUST CATCH A COCONUT, THEN SPLIT AND STRIP THE HUSK IN THE FASTEST TIME!
TIME TO TEST MY DEXTERITY! CATCH, SPIKE, TWIST, PEEL--GOT IT!
GO!
OKAY, I'M HERE! DROP ME A COCONUT!
I CAN'T!
WHY?!
YOUR BASKET ISN'T EMPTY!
!
HEIHEI, THERE ARE BETTER PLACES TO NAP!
HEADS UP!
THOK
?

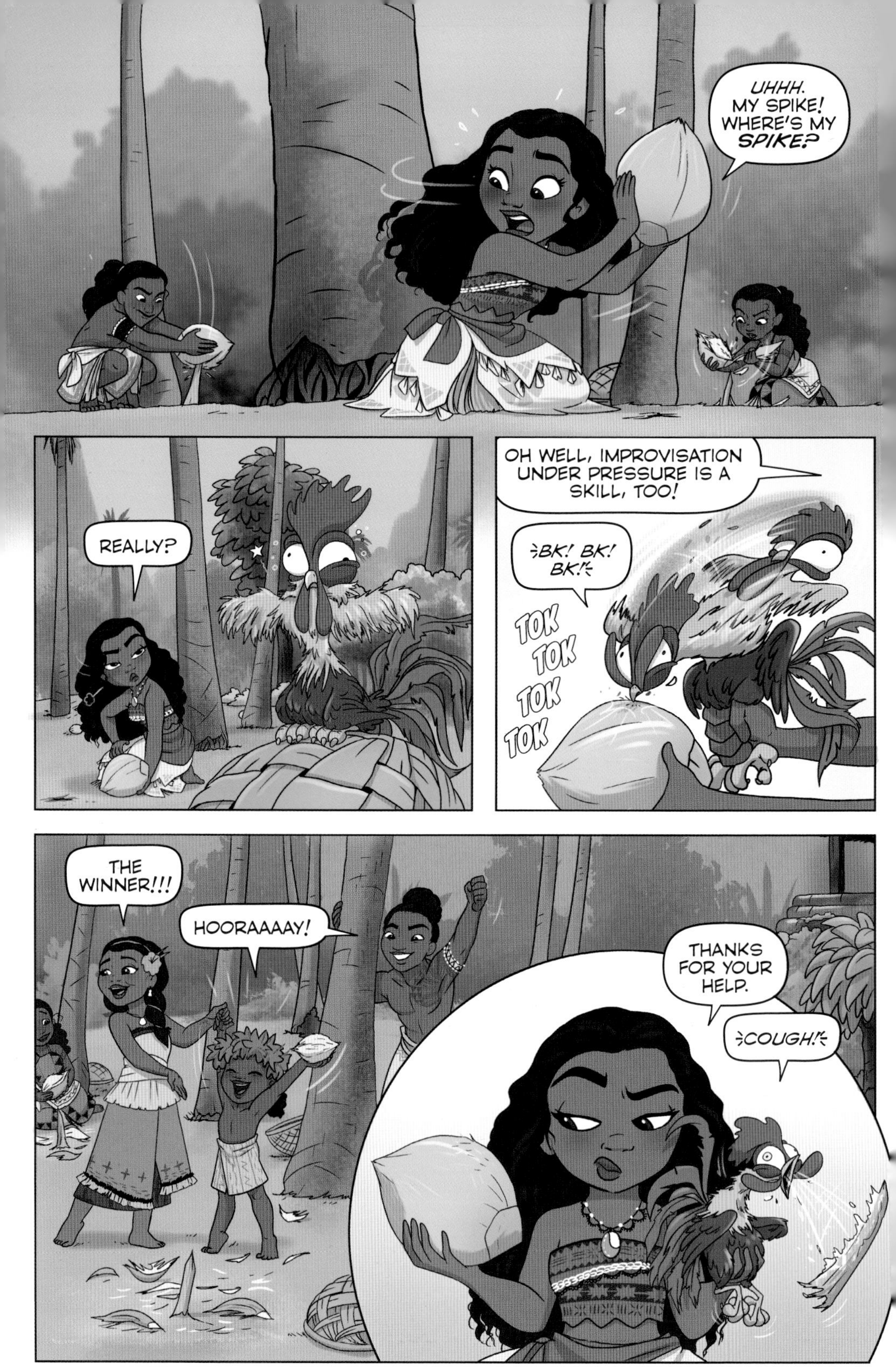
UHHH. MY SPIKE! WHERE'S MY SPIKE?
REALLY?
OH WELL, IMPROVISATION UNDER PRESSURE IS A SKILL, TOO!
BK! BK! BK!
TOK TOK TOK TOK
THE WINNER!!!
HOORAAAAY!
THANKS FOR YOUR HELP.
COUGH!

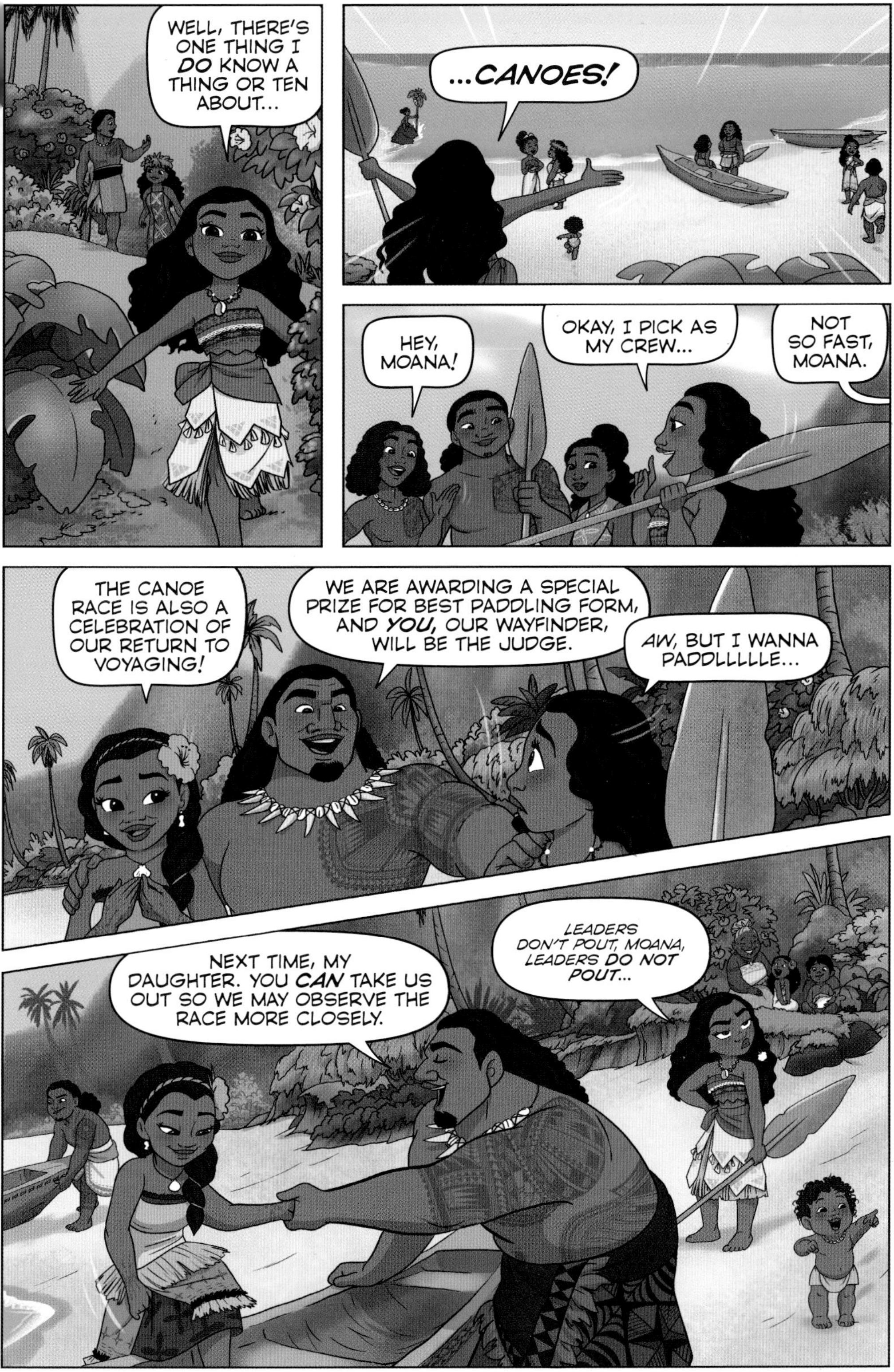
WELL, THERE'S ONE THING I *DO* KNOW A THING OR TEN ABOUT...
...CANOES!
HEY, MOANA!
OKAY, I PICK AS MY CREW...
NOT SO FAST, MOANA.
THE CANOE RACE IS ALSO A CELEBRATION OF OUR RETURN TO VOYAGING!
WE ARE AWARDING A SPECIAL PRIZE FOR BEST PADDLING FORM, AND *YOU,* OUR WAYFINDER, WILL BE THE JUDGE.
AW, BUT I WANNA PADDLLLLLE...
NEXT TIME, MY DAUGHTER. YOU *CAN* TAKE US OUT SO WE MAY OBSERVE THE RACE MORE CLOSELY.
LEADERS DON'T POUT, MOANA, LEADERS DO NOT POUT...

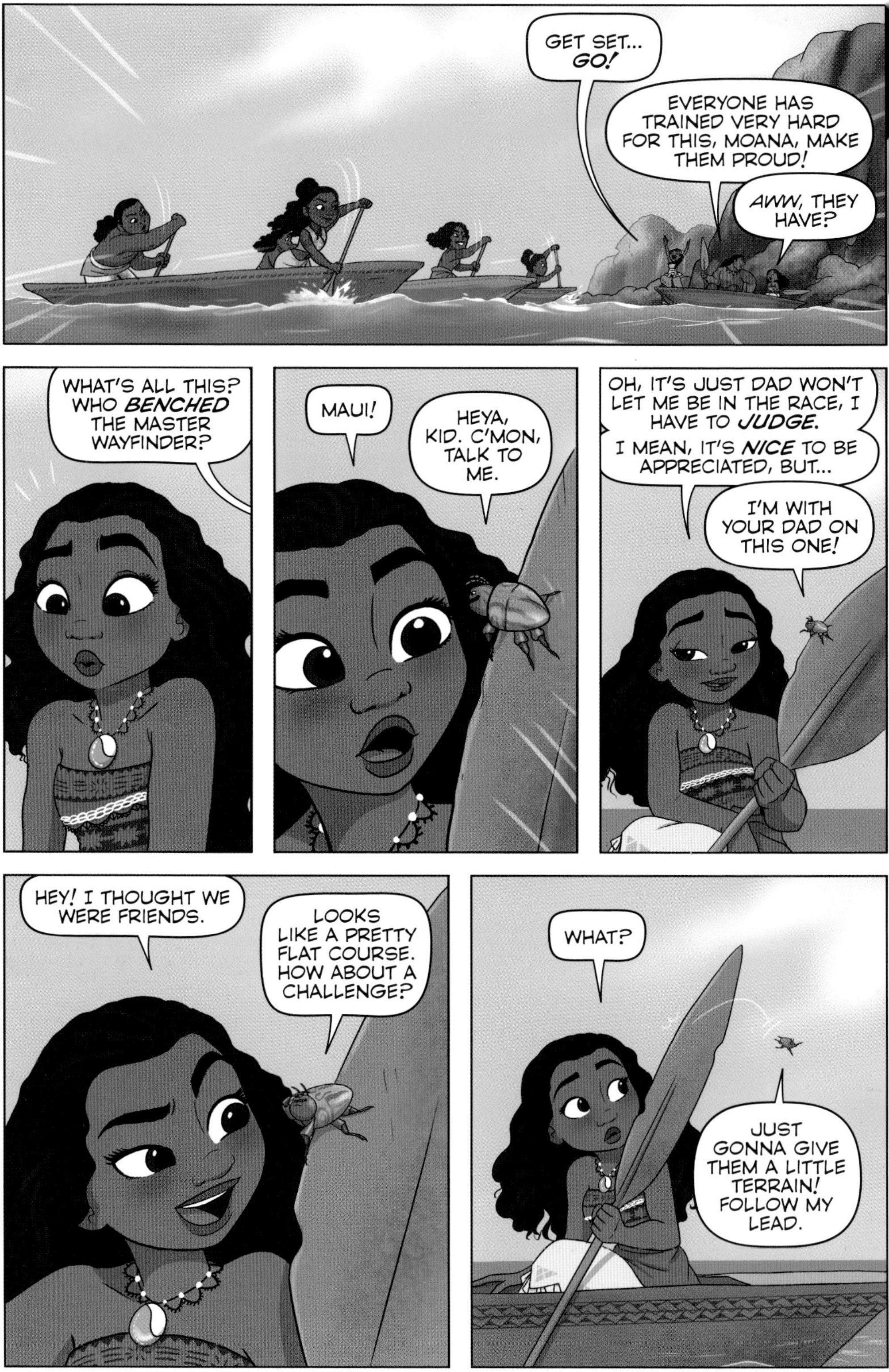
GET SET... *GO!*
EVERYONE HAS TRAINED VERY HARD FOR THIS, MOANA, MAKE THEM PROUD!
AWW, THEY HAVE?
WHAT'S ALL THIS? WHO *BENCHED* THE MASTER WAYFINDER?
MAUI!
HEYA, KID. C'MON, TALK TO ME.
OH, IT'S JUST DAD WON'T LET ME BE IN THE RACE, I HAVE TO *JUDGE*.
I MEAN, IT'S *NICE* TO BE APPRECIATED, BUT...
I'M WITH YOUR DAD ON THIS ONE!
HEY! I THOUGHT WE WERE FRIENDS.
LOOKS LIKE A PRETTY FLAT COURSE. HOW ABOUT A CHALLENGE?
WHAT?
JUST GONNA GIVE THEM A LITTLE TERRAIN! FOLLOW MY LEAD.

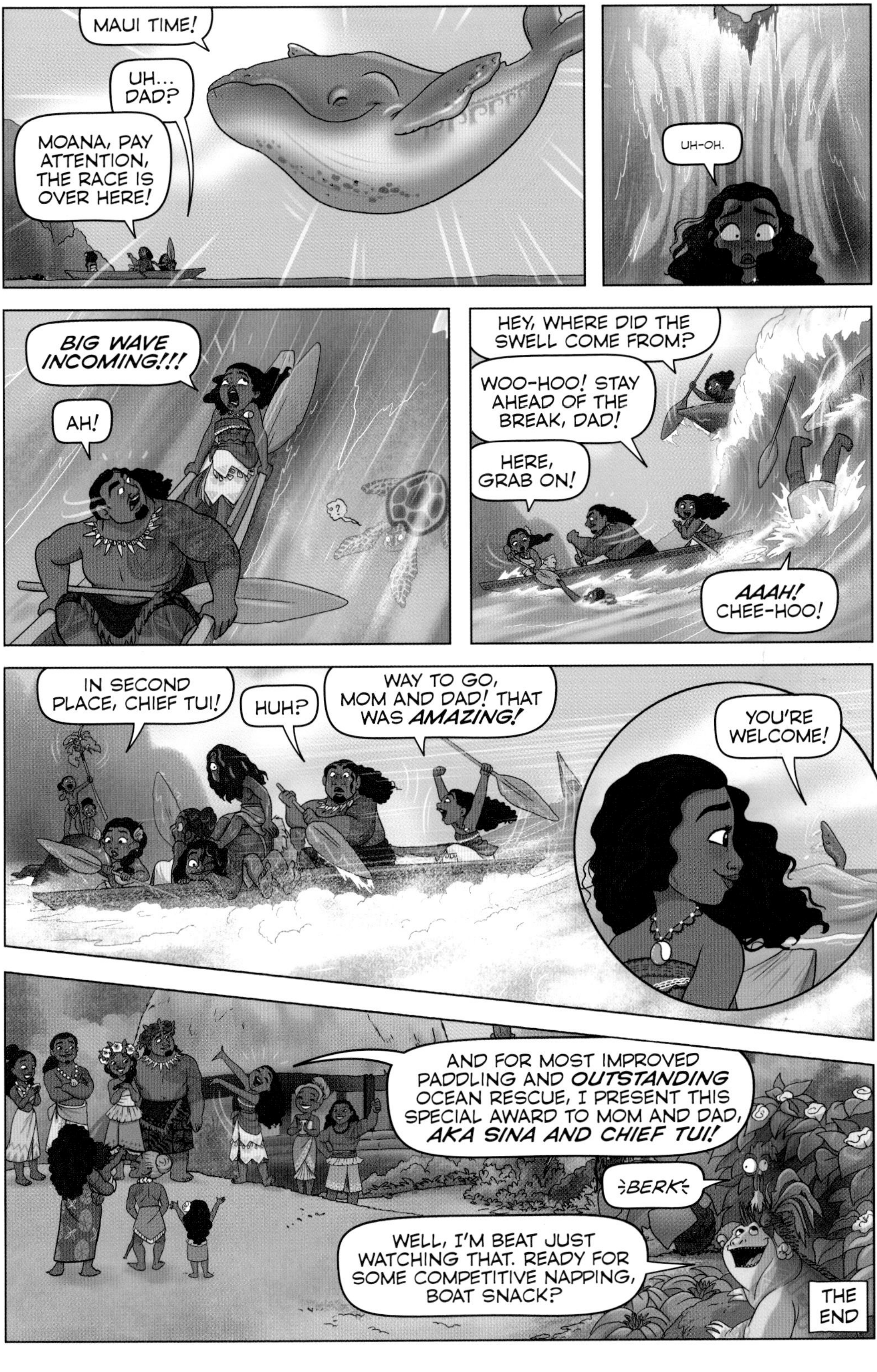
MAUI TIME!
UH... DAD?
MOANA, PAY ATTENTION, THE RACE IS OVER HERE!
UH-OH.
BIG WAVE INCOMING!!!
AH!
HEY, WHERE DID THE SWELL COME FROM?
WOO-HOO! STAY AHEAD OF THE BREAK, DAD!
HERE, GRAB ON!
AAAH! CHEE-HOO!
IN SECOND PLACE, CHIEF TUI!
HUH?
WAY TO GO, MOM AND DAD! THAT WAS AMAZING!
YOU'RE WELCOME!
AND FOR MOST IMPROVED PADDLING AND OUTSTANDING OCEAN RESCUE, I PRESENT THIS SPECIAL AWARD TO MOM AND DAD, AKA SINA AND CHIEF TUI!
BERK
WELL, I'M BEAT JUST WATCHING THAT. READY FOR SOME COMPETITIVE NAPPING, BOAT SNACK?
THE END

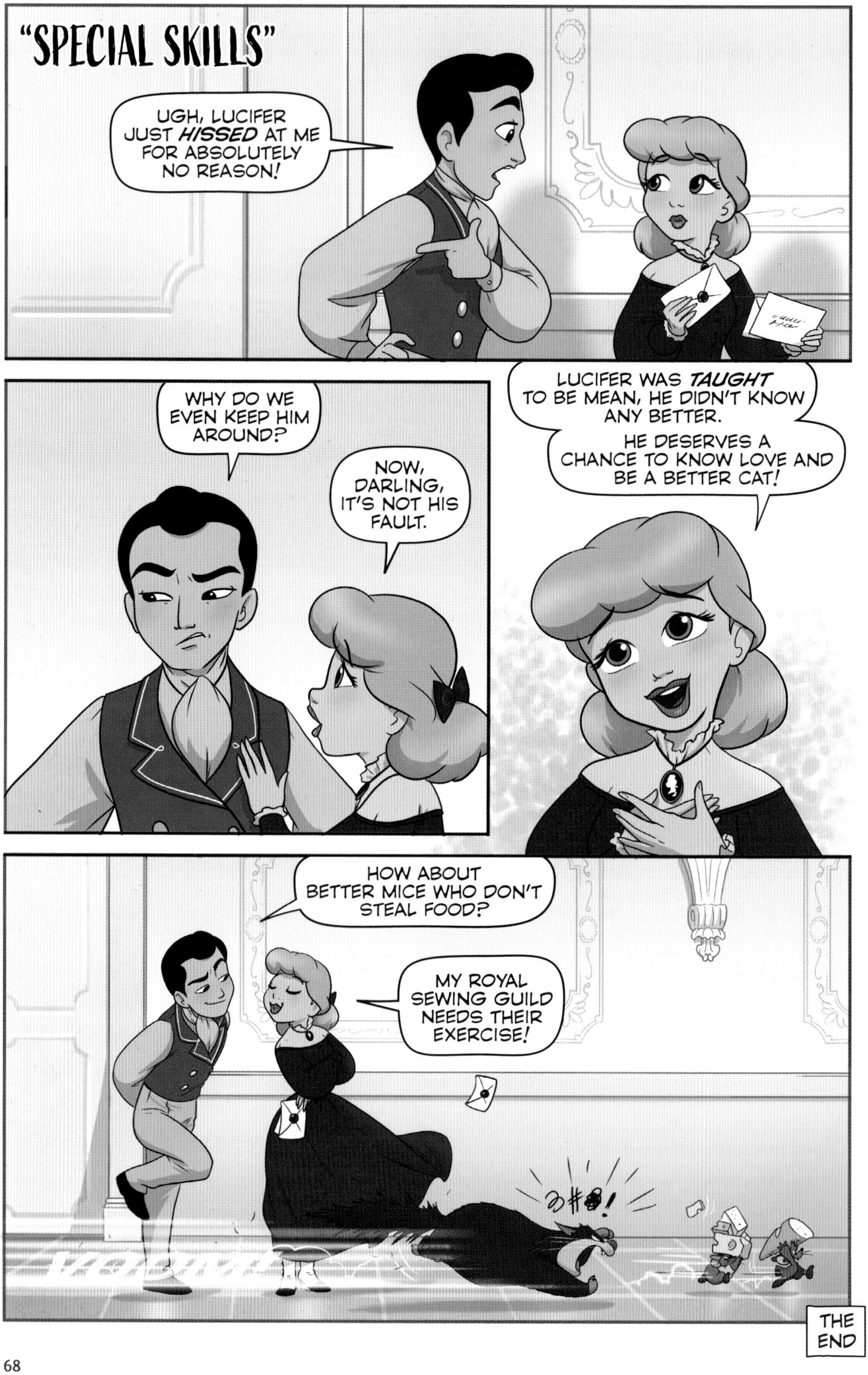
"SPECIAL SKILLS"
UGH, LUCIFER JUST HISSED AT ME FOR ABSOLUTELY NO REASON!
WHY DO WE EVEN KEEP HIM AROUND?
NOW, DARLING, IT'S NOT HIS FAULT.
LUCIFER WAS TAUGHT TO BE MEAN, HE DIDN'T KNOW ANY BETTER.
HE DESERVES A CHANCE TO KNOW LOVE AND BE A BETTER CAT!
HOW ABOUT BETTER MICE WHO DON'T STEAL FOOD?
MY ROYAL SEWING GUILD NEEDS THEIR EXERCISE!
THE END

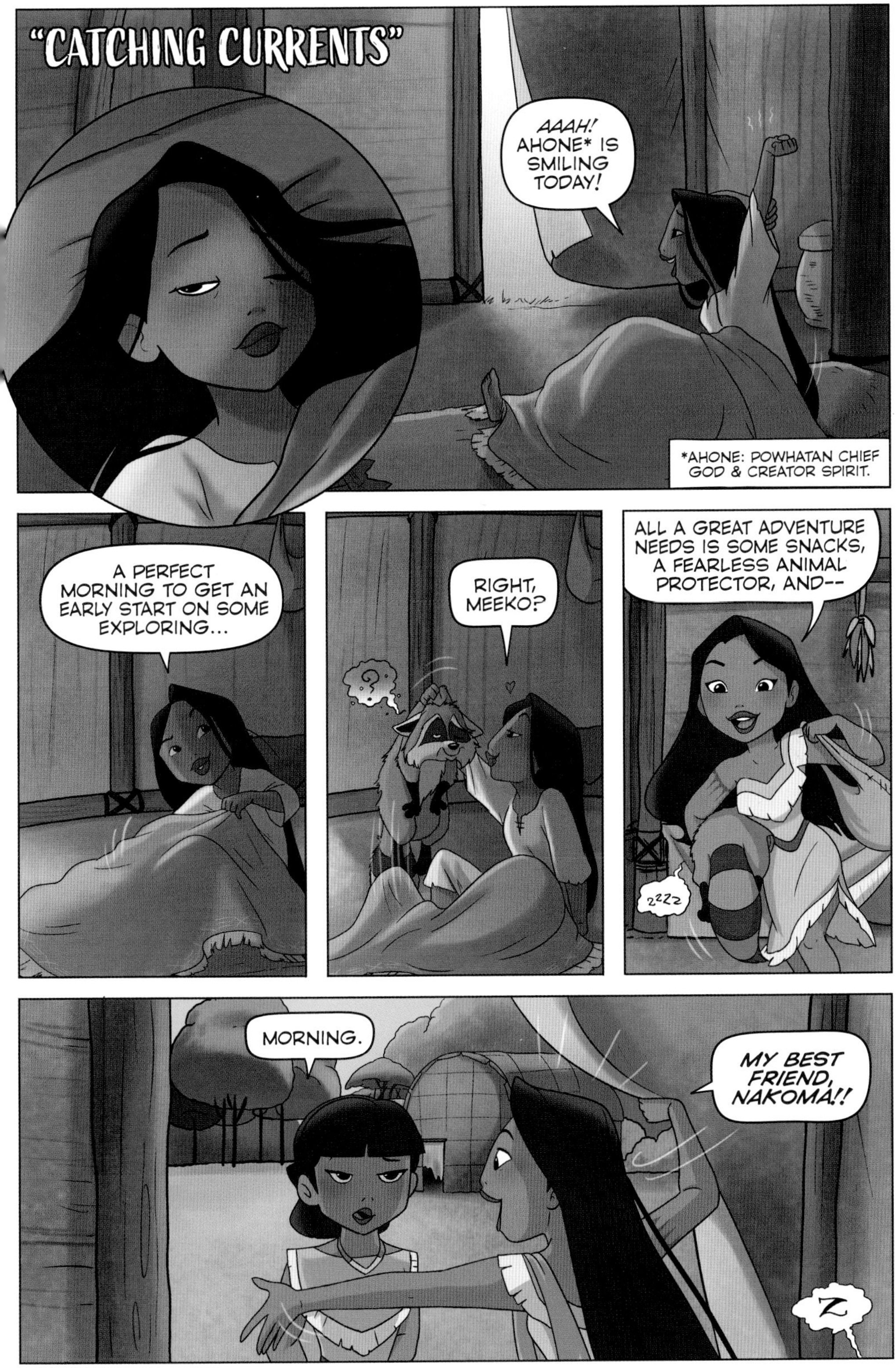
"CATCHING CURRENTS"
AAAH! AHONE* IS SMILING TODAY!
*AHONE: POWHATAN CHIEF GOD & CREATOR SPIRIT.
A PERFECT MORNING TO GET AN EARLY START ON SOME EXPLORING...
RIGHT, MEEKO?
?
ALL A GREAT ADVENTURE NEEDS IS SOME SNACKS, A FEARLESS ANIMAL PROTECTOR, AND--
ZZZZ
MORNING.
MY BEST FRIEND, NAKOMA!!
Z

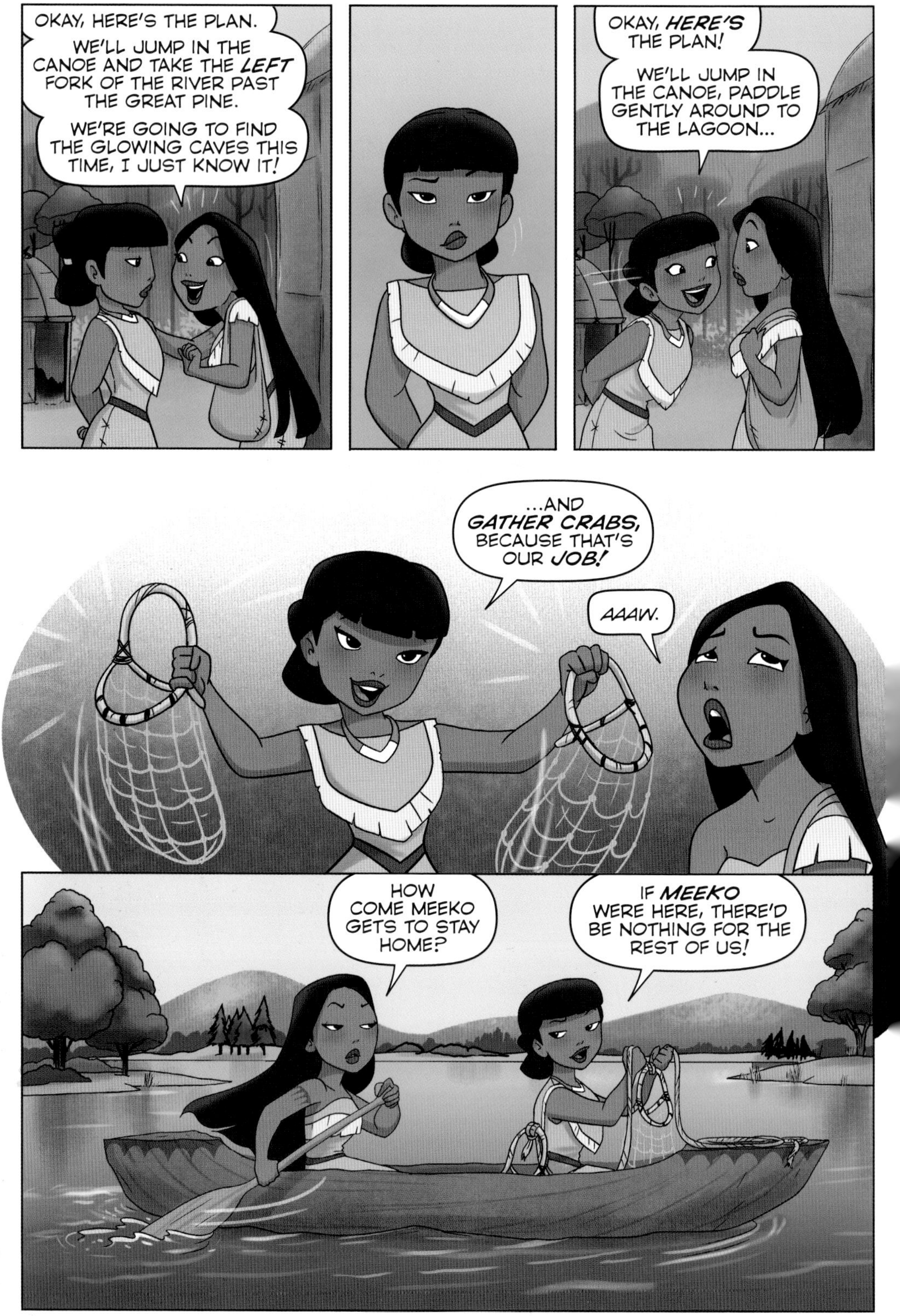
OKAY, HERE'S THE PLAN.
WE'LL JUMP IN THE CANOE AND TAKE THE *LEFT* FORK OF THE RIVER PAST THE GREAT PINE.
WE'RE GOING TO FIND THE GLOWING CAVES THIS TIME, I JUST KNOW IT!
OKAY, *HERE'S* THE PLAN!
WE'LL JUMP IN THE CANOE, PADDLE GENTLY AROUND TO THE LAGOON...
...AND *GATHER CRABS,* BECAUSE THAT'S OUR *JOB!*
AAAW.
HOW COME MEEKO GETS TO STAY HOME?
IF *MEEKO* WERE HERE, THERE'D BE NOTHING FOR THE REST OF US!

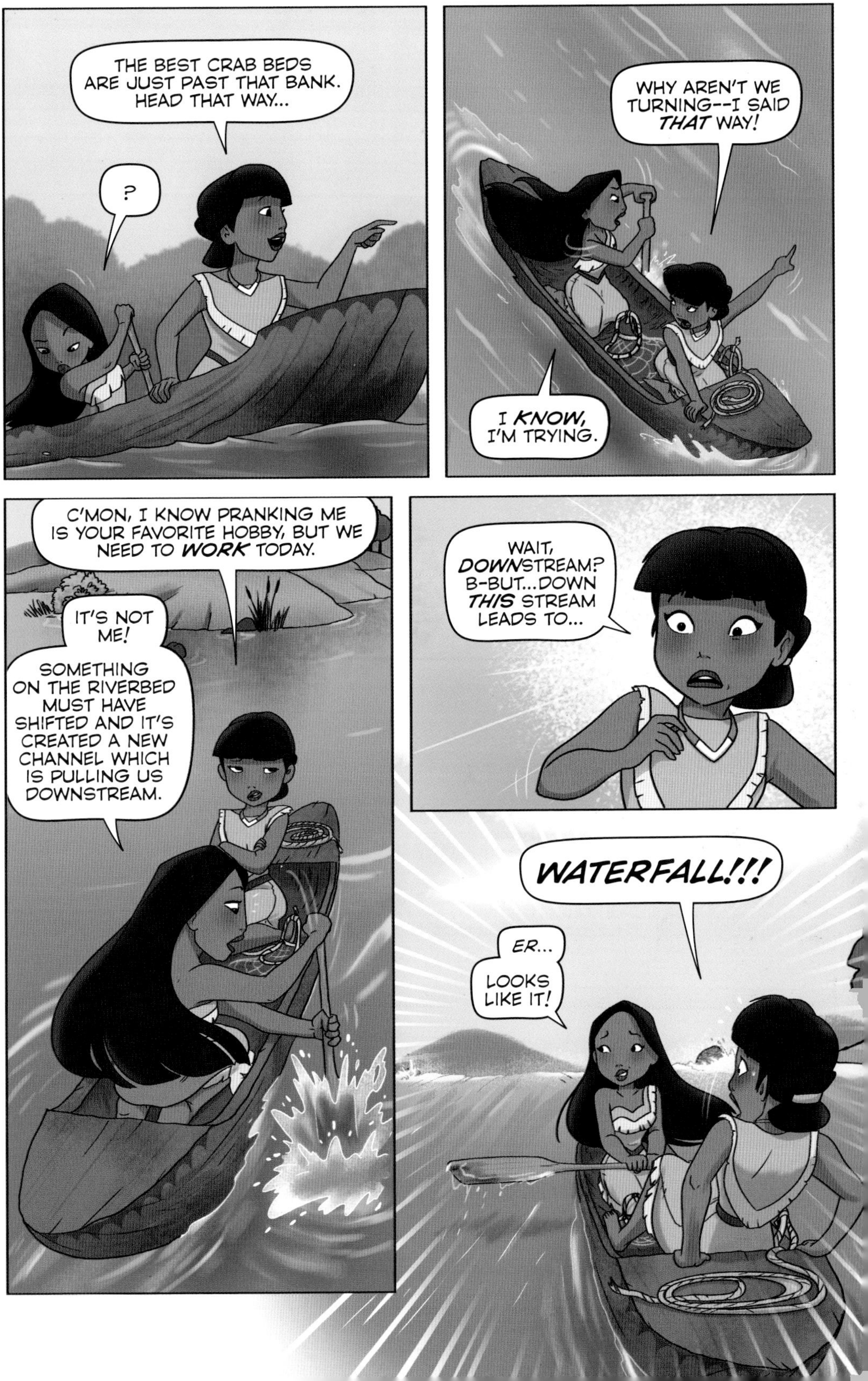
THE BEST CRAB BEDS ARE JUST PAST THAT BANK. HEAD THAT WAY...
?
WHY AREN'T WE TURNING--I SAID THAT WAY!
I KNOW, I'M TRYING.
C'MON, I KNOW PRANKING ME IS YOUR FAVORITE HOBBY, BUT WE NEED TO WORK TODAY.
IT'S NOT ME!
SOMETHING ON THE RIVERBED MUST HAVE SHIFTED AND IT'S CREATED A NEW CHANNEL WHICH IS PULLING US DOWNSTREAM.
WAIT, DOWNSTREAM? B-BUT...DOWN THIS STREAM LEADS TO...
WATERFALL!!!
ER...
LOOKS LIKE IT!

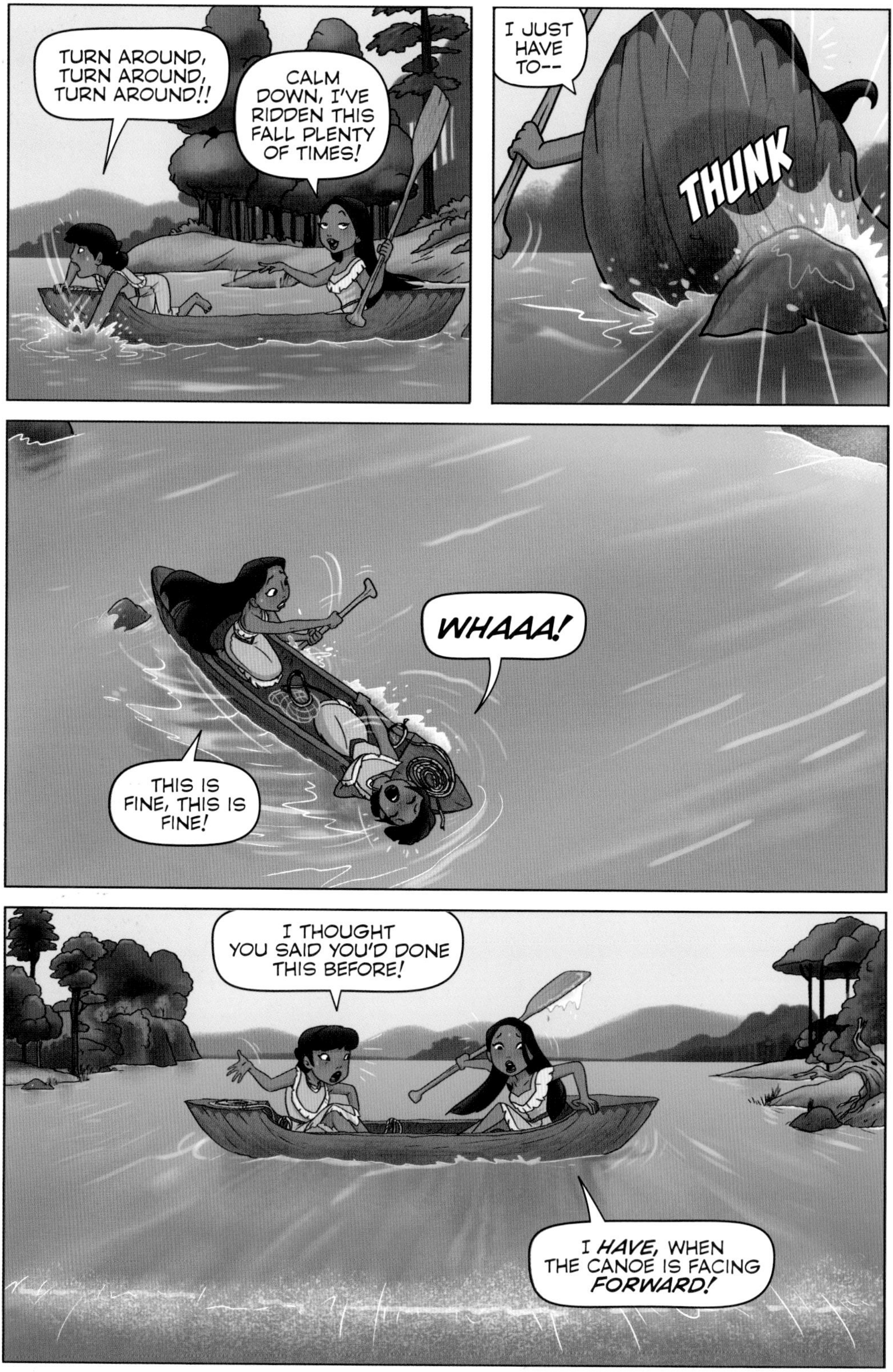
TURN AROUND, TURN AROUND, TURN AROUND!!
CALM DOWN, I'VE RIDDEN THIS FALL PLENTY OF TIMES!
I JUST HAVE TO--
THUNK
WHAAA!
THIS IS FINE, THIS IS FINE!
I THOUGHT YOU SAID YOU'D DONE THIS BEFORE!
I *HAVE,* WHEN THE CANOE IS FACING *FORWARD!*

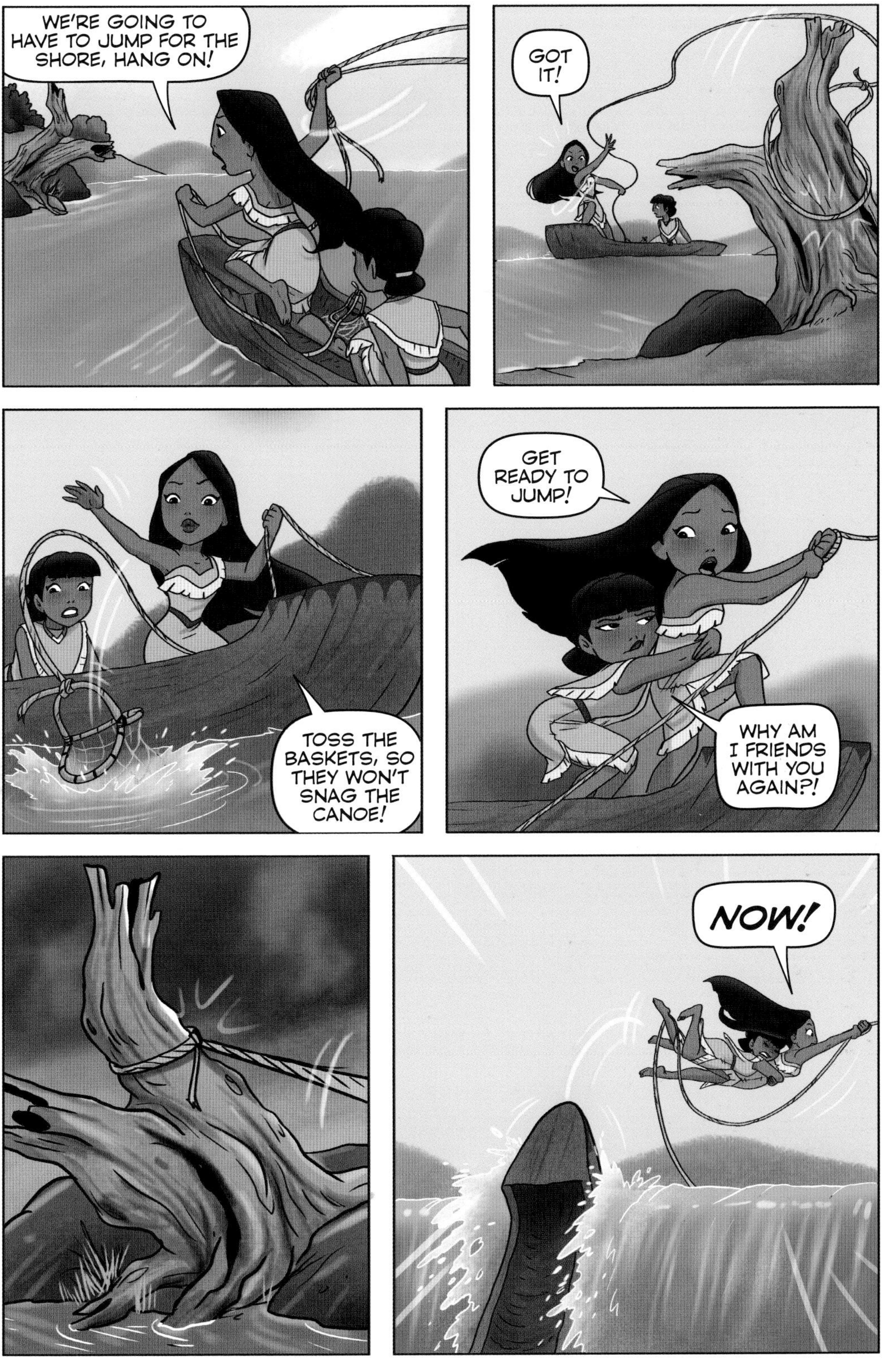
WE'RE GOING TO HAVE TO JUMP FOR THE SHORE, HANG ON!
GOT IT!
TOSS THE BASKETS, SO THEY WON'T SNAG THE CANOE!
GET READY TO JUMP!
WHY AM I FRIENDS WITH YOU AGAIN?!
NOW!

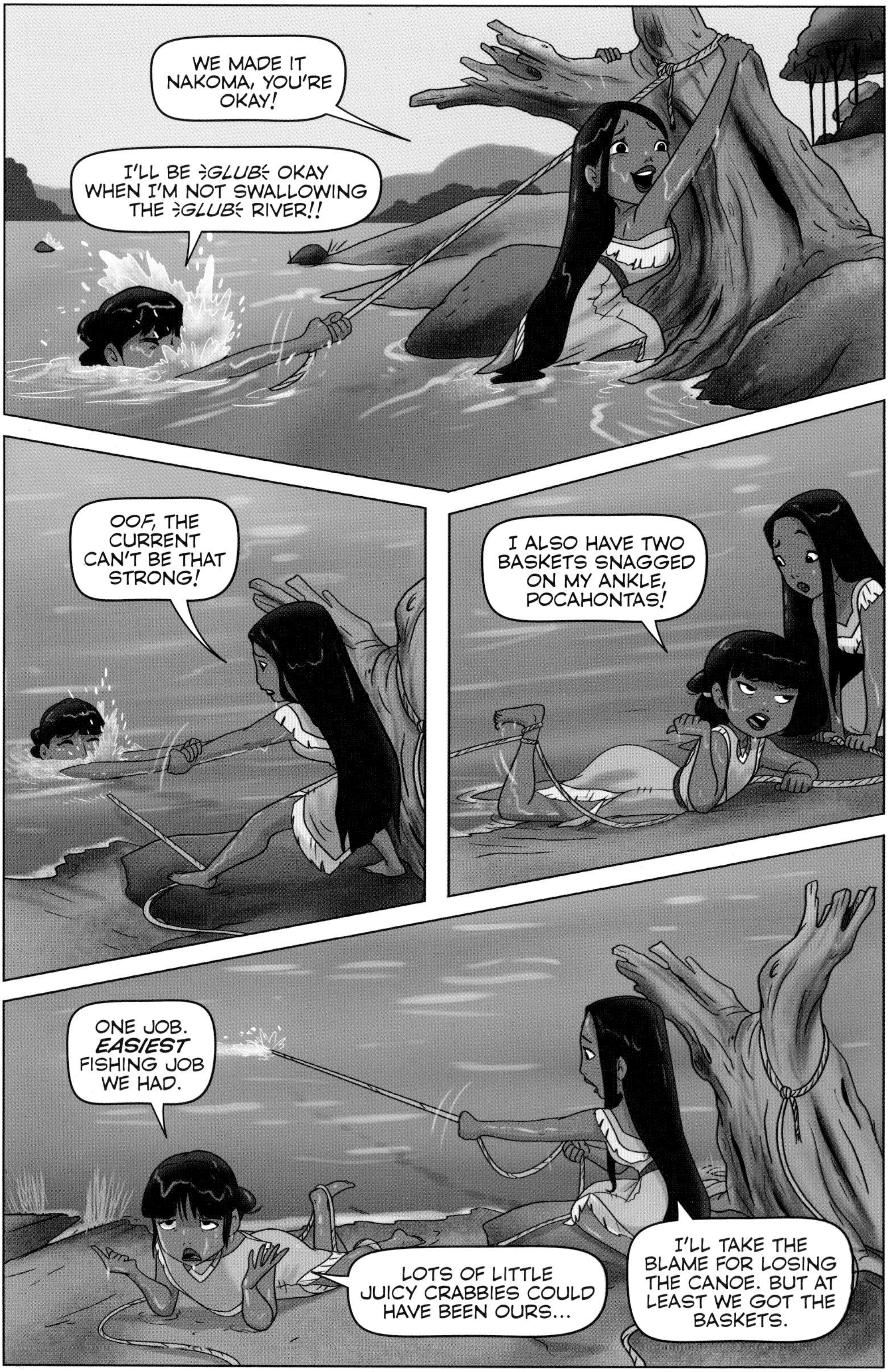
WE MADE IT NAKOMA, YOU'RE OKAY!
I'LL BE ⦒GLUB⦑ OKAY WHEN I'M NOT SWALLOWING THE ⦒GLUB⦑ RIVER!!
OOF, THE CURRENT CAN'T BE THAT STRONG!
I ALSO HAVE TWO BASKETS SNAGGED ON MY ANKLE, POCAHONTAS!
ONE JOB. ***EASIEST*** FISHING JOB WE HAD.
LOTS OF LITTLE JUICY CRABBIES COULD HAVE BEEN OURS...
I'LL TAKE THE BLAME FOR LOSING THE CANOE. BUT AT LEAST WE GOT THE BASKETS.

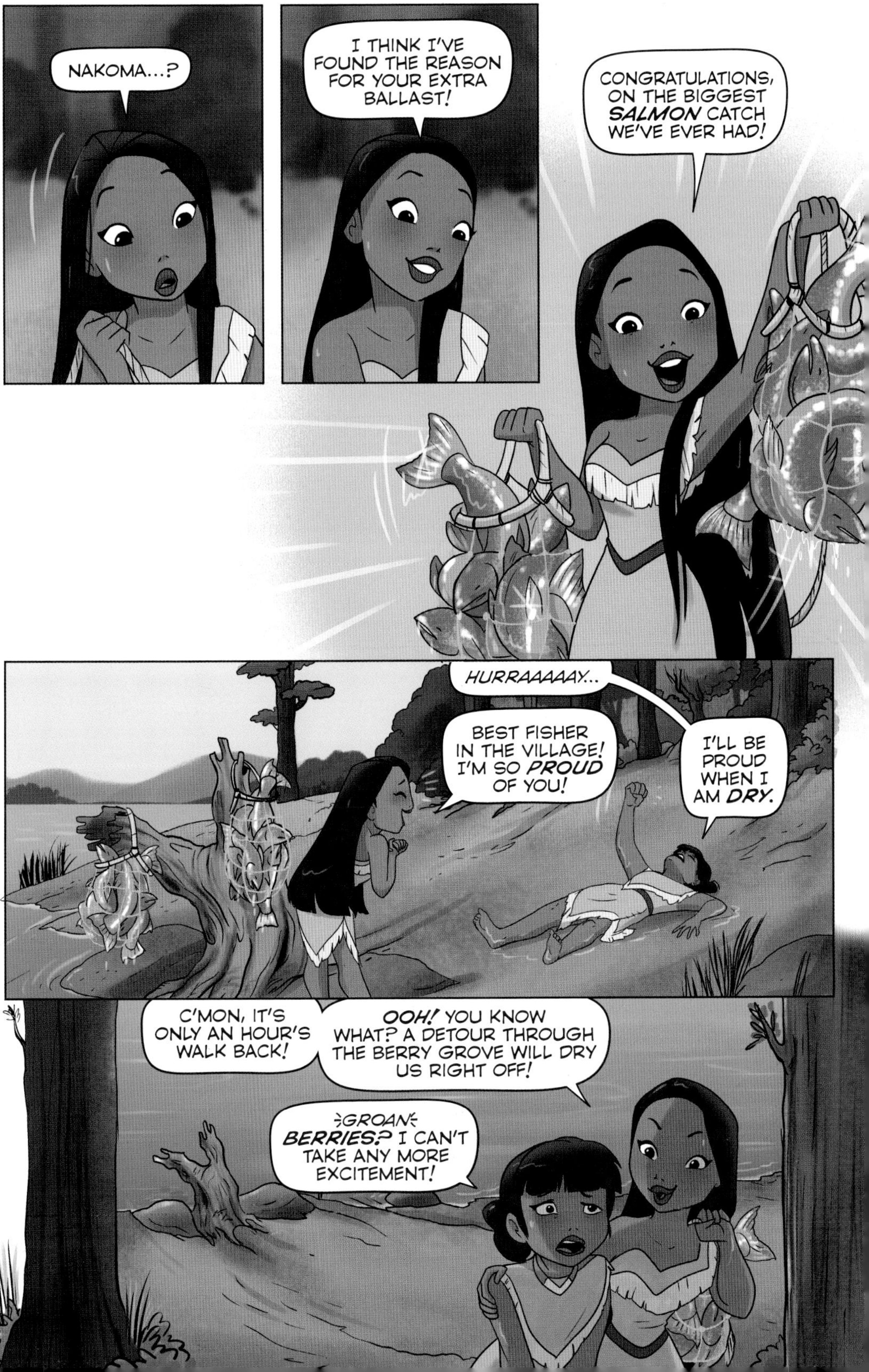
NAKOMA...?
I THINK I'VE FOUND THE REASON FOR YOUR EXTRA BALLAST!
CONGRATULATIONS, ON THE BIGGEST SALMON CATCH WE'VE EVER HAD!
HURRAAAAAY...
BEST FISHER IN THE VILLAGE! I'M SO PROUD OF YOU!
I'LL BE PROUD WHEN I AM DRY.
C'MON, IT'S ONLY AN HOUR'S WALK BACK!
OOH! YOU KNOW WHAT? A DETOUR THROUGH THE BERRY GROVE WILL DRY US RIGHT OFF!
GROAN
BERRIES? I CAN'T TAKE ANY MORE EXCITEMENT!

SEE, WASN'T THAT *SO* MUCH MORE INTERESTING THAN CRABS?

WHEN ONE HOUR'S WALK BECAME *THREE*, THE INTEREST WANED A BIT.

DAUGHTER! YOU'VE BEEN GONE AN AWFULLY LONG TIME JUST TO GATHER CRABS.

WELL, WE KIND OF GOT A LITTLE SIDETRACKED, YOU SEE, WE--

SHE LOST THE CANOE DOWN THE FALLS.

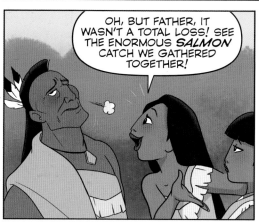

OH, BUT FATHER, IT WASN'T A TOTAL LOSS! SEE THE ENORMOUS *SALMON* CATCH WE GATHERED TOGETHER!

HOW INTERESTING, FISH MADE OF AIR.

WHAT?

MEEKO, NO!!!

IF I CATCH HIM, THE CRABS CAN *HAVE* HIM!

THE END

DARK HORSE BOOKS

president and publisher
Mike Richardson

editor
Freddye Miller

assistant editor
Judy Khuu

designer
Anita Magaña

digital art technician
Samantha Hummer

Neil Hankerson *Executive Vice President* ✦ **Tom Weddle** *Chief Financial Officer* ✦ **Randy Stradley** *Vice President of Publishing* ✦ **Nick McWhorter** *Chief Business Development Officer* ✦ **Dale LaFountain** *Chief Information Officer* ✦ **Matt Parkinson** *Vice President of Marketing* ✦ **Vanessa Todd-Holmes** *Vice President of Production and Scheduling* ✦ **Mark Bernardi** *Vice President of Book Trade and Digital Sales* ✦ **Ken Lizzi** *General Counsel* ✦ **Dave Marshall** *Editor in Chief* ✦ **Davey Estrada** *Editorial Director* ✦ **Chris Warner** *Senior Books Editor* ✦ **Cary Grazzini** *Director of Specialty Projects* ✦ **Lia Ribacchi** *Art Director* ✦ **Matt Dryer** *Director of Digital Art and Prepress* ✦ **Michael Gombos** *Senior Director of Licensed Publications* ✦ **Kari Yadro** *Director of Custom Programs* ✦ **Kari Torson** *Director of International Licensing* ✦ **Sean Brice** *Director of Trade Sales*

DISNEY PUBLISHING WORLDWIDE GLOBAL MAGAZINES, COMICS AND PARTWORKS
PUBLISHER Lynn Waggoner ✦ **EDITORIAL TEAM Bianca Coletti** *(Director, Magazines)*, **Guido Frazzini** *(Director, Comics)*, **Carlotta Quattrocolo** *(Executive Editor)*, **Stefano Ambrosio** *(Executive Editor, New IP)*, **Camilla Vedove** *(Senior Manager, Editorial Development)*, **Behnoosh Khalili** *(Senior Editor)*, **Julie Dorris** *(Senior Editor)*, **Mina Riazi** *(Assistant Editor)*, **Gabriela Capasso** *(Assistant Editor)* ✦ **DESIGN Enrico Soave** *(Senior Designer)* ✦ **ART Ken Shue** *(VP, Global Art)*, **Manny Mederos** *(Senior Illustration Manager, Comics and Magazines)*, **Roberto Santillo** *(Creative Director)*, **Marco Ghiglione** *(Creative Manager)*, **Stefano Attardi** *(Illustration Manager)* ✦ **PORTFOLIO MANAGEMENT Olivia Ciancarelli** *(Director)* ✦ **BUSINESS & MARKETING Mariantonietta Galla** *(Senior Manager, Franchise)*, **Virpi Korhonen** *(Editorial Manager)*

DISNEY PRINCESS: MAKE WAY FOR FUN

Published by Dark Horse Books
A division of Dark Horse Comics LLC
10956 SE Main Street
Milwaukie, OR 97222

DarkHorse.com
To find a comics shop in your area, visit comicshoplocator.com

First edition: January 2021
Ebook ISBN 978-1-50671-678-7 | Trade Paperback ISBN 978-1-50671-673-2

1 3 5 7 9 10 8 6 4 2
Printed in China

Fun Disney Princess stories for all ages!

LOOKING FOR BOOKS FOR YOUNGER READERS?

$7.99 each!

EACH VOLUME INCLUDES A SECTION OF FUN ACTIVITIES!

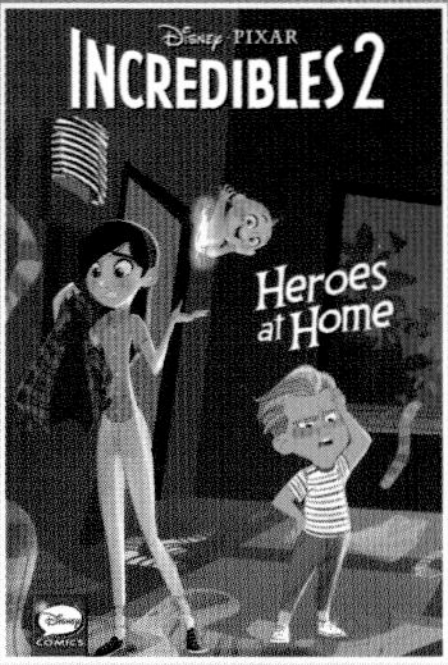

Disney PIXAR
INCREDIBLES 2
Heroes at Home

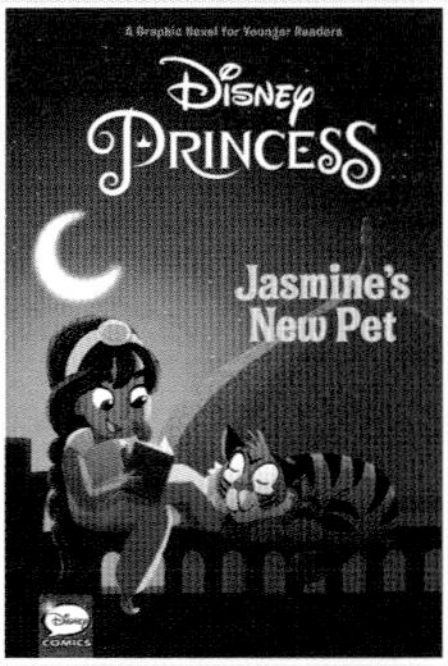

A Graphic Novel for Younger Readers
Disney PRINCESS
Jasmine's New Pet

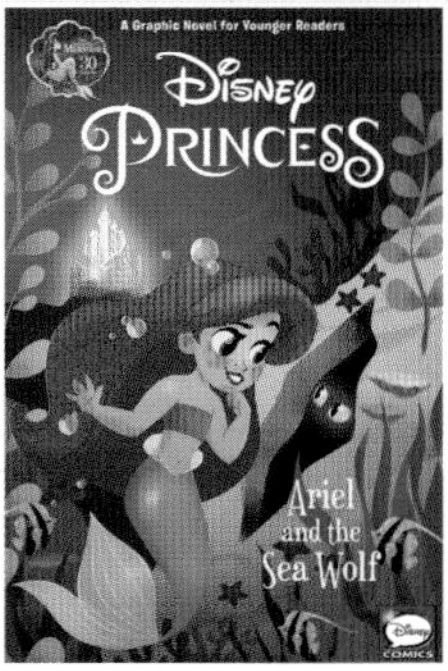

A Graphic Novel for Younger Readers
Disney PRINCESS
Ariel and the Sea Wolf

DISNEY•PIXAR INCREDIBLES 2: HEROES AT HOME
ISBN 978-1-50670-943-7
Being part of a Super family means helping out at home, too. Can Violet and Dash pick up groceries and secretly stop some bad guys? And can they clean up the house while Jack-Jack is "sleeping"?

DISNEY PRINCESS: JASMINE'S NEW PET
ISBN 978-1-50671-052-5
Jasmine has a new pet tiger, Rajah, but he's not quite ready for palace life. Will she be able to train the young cub before the Sultan finds him another home?

DISNEY PRINCESS: ARIEL AND THE SEA WOLF
ISBN 978-1-50671-203-1
Ariel accidentally drops a bracelet into a cave that supposedly contains a dangerous creature. Her curiosity implores her to enter, and what she finds turns her quest for a bracelet into a quest for truth.

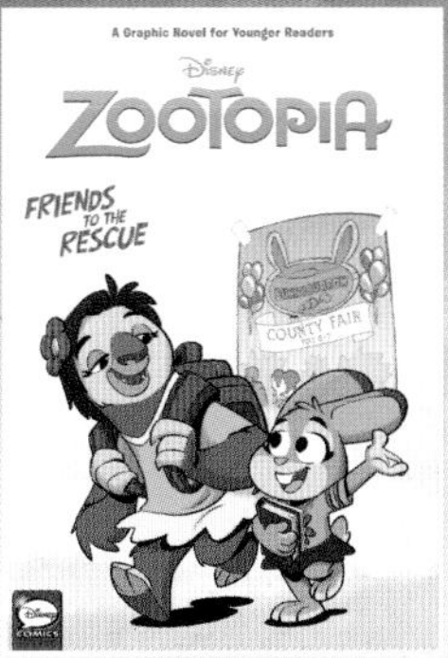

A Graphic Novel for Younger Readers
Disney ZOOTOPIA
FRIENDS TO THE RESCUE
COUNTY FAIR

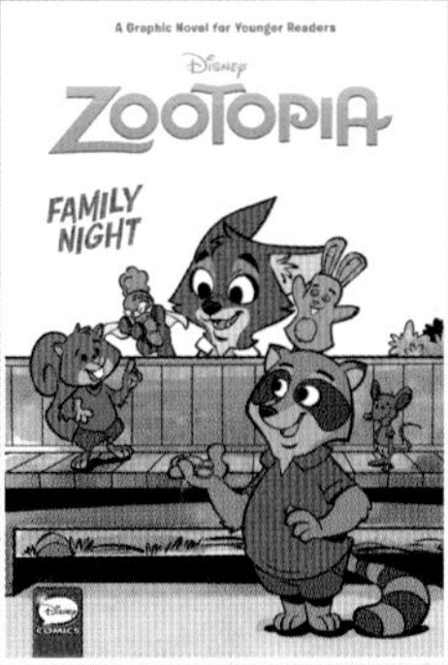

A Graphic Novel for Younger Readers
Disney ZOOTOPIA
FAMILY NIGHT

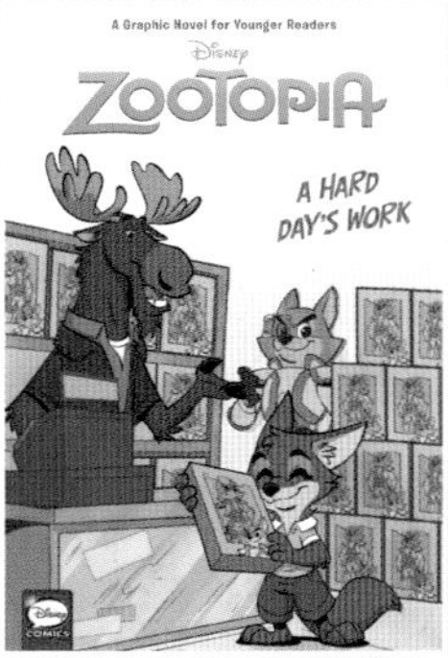

A Graphic Novel for Younger Readers
Disney ZOOTOPIA
A HARD DAY'S WORK

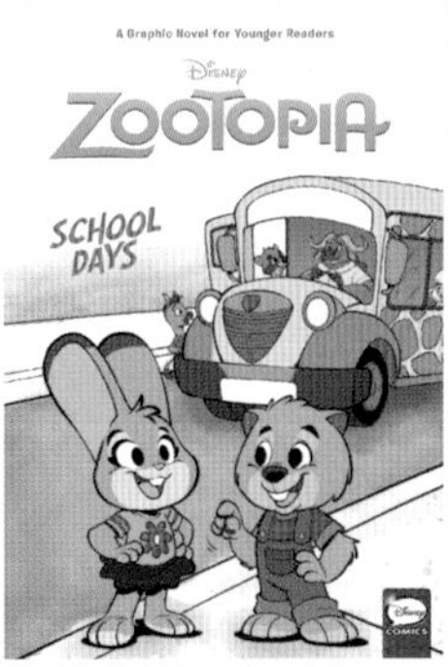

A Graphic Novel for Younger Readers
Disney ZOOTOPIA
SCHOOL DAYS

DISNEY ZOOTOPIA: FRIENDS TO THE RESCUE
ISBN 978-1-50671-054-9

DISNEY ZOOTOPIA: FAMILY NIGHT
ISBN 978-1-50671-053-2

DISNEY ZOOTOPIA: A HARD DAY'S WORK
ISBN 978-1-50671-206-2

DISNEY ZOOTOPIA: SCHOOL DAYS
ISBN 978-1-50671-205-5
Join young Judy Hopps as she uses wit and bravery to solve mysteries, conundrums, and more! And quick-thinking young Nick Wilde won't be stopped from achieving his goals—where there's a will, there's a way!

AVAILABLE AT YOUR LOCAL COMICS SHOP OR BOOKSTORE! TO FIND A COMICS SHOP IN YOUR AREA, VISIT COMICSHOPLOCATOR.COM

For more information or to order direct, visit DarkHorse.com

Looking for Disney *Frozen*?

$10.99 each!

Disney
FROZEN
Breaking Boundaries

Disney Frozen: Breaking Boundaries
978-1-50671-051-8

Anna, Elsa, and friends have a quest to fulfill, mysteries to solve, and peace to restore!

Disney
FROZEN
Reunion Road

Disney Frozen: Reunion Road
978-1-50671-270-3

Elsa and Anna gather friends and family for an unforgettable trip to a harvest festival in the neighboring kingdom of Snoob!

Disney
FROZEN
The Hero Within

Disney Frozen: The Hero Within
978-1-50671-269-7

Anna, Elsa, Kristoff, Sven, Olaf, and new friend Hedda, deal with bullies and the harsh environment of the Forbidden Land!

Disney
FROZEN
True Treasure

Disney Frozen: True Treasure
978-1-50671-705-0

A lead-in story to Disney *Frozen 2*. Elsa and Anna embark on an adventure searching for clues to uncover a lost message from their mother.

Disney
FROZEN
ADVENTURES
Flurries of Fun

Disney Frozen Adventures: Flurries of Fun
978-1-50671-470-7

Disney
FROZEN
ADVENTURES
Snowy Stories

Disney Frozen Adventures: Snowy Stories
978-1-50671-471-4

Disney
FROZEN
ADVENTURES
Ice and Magic

Disney Frozen Adventures: Ice and Magic
978-1-50671-472-1

Collections of short comics stories expanding on the world of Disney *Frozen*!

AVAILABLE AT YOUR LOCAL COMICS SHOP OR BOOKSTORE!
TO FIND A COMICS SHOP IN YOUR AREA, VISIT COMICSHOPLOCATOR.COM

For more information or to order direct, visit DarkHorse.com

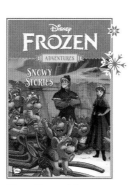